Dear Reader,

I like to write about heroines who have a tender heart and gentle soul, while at the same time are determinedly independent with a strong moral fiber. However, no matter how strong our moral fiber is, momentary weaknesses and making mistakes is part of being human. It's how we handle those weaknesses and mistakes that counts in the end. This was the premise behind the book.

Like Father, Like Son ranks among my most favorite of those I have written. I became very attached to Rebecca, Tanner, Michael and the rest of the cast of characters. I hope you enjoy their story as much I enjoyed writing it.

Sincerely,

Elizabeth August

GREATEST TEXAS LOVE STORIES OF ALL TIME

★

GREATEST
TEXAS LOVE STORIES
OF ALL TIME

Like Father,
Like Son
Elizabeth August

Lone Star Lullabies

▼
Silhouette Books
™
Published by Silhouette Books
America's Publisher of Contemporary Romance

SILHOUETTE BOOKS

ISBN 0-373-65228-3

LIKE FATHER, LIKE SON

Printed in U.S.A.

ELIZABETH AUGUST

lives in the mountains of North Carolina with her husband, Doug. Her three sons are now grown and have left home in pursuit of their careers. She and her husband are playing more golf and bridge. Doug's game is improving. Elizabeth is enjoying being outdoors and she loves the beauty of the golf courses. As a cancer survivor she plays in tournaments that support cancer research and wishes to send out her very deepest wishes to all of her readers who have survived and those who are now fighting the various forms of this disease.

To all those romantics who, like myself,
believe that true love will survive despite
the obstacles that many times get in the way.

Chapter One

Rebecca surfaced in a torrent of pain. Her head throbbed and, when she attempted to move, every inch of her cried out in protest. Her mouth felt as if it were filled with cotton balls, and only a strange scratchy sound issued from somewhere at the back of her throat when she tried to speak.

Janie Masters, the nurse in charge of the intensive-care unit for the night shift, stood beside the bed. Glancing at the heart monitor, she noted that, although the rhythm was weak, it was steady. A frown darkened her countenance. It didn't seem fair that the drunk driver who had placed this pleasant-featured, twenty-seven-year-old woman on the threshold of death had escaped with only a few scratches. "You're in a hospital," Janie informed her patient in reassuring tones. "You're going to be just fine," she added. That wasn't something she could guarantee but she liked to say it. It made her feel more encouraged.

In response, there was a confused, vacant look in the brown eyes that stared back at her, and Janie held her breath. She hated moments like this.

In addition to extensive internal injuries, the accident had left Rebecca Worthen with several cracked ribs plus cuts and contusions. Her most serious injury, however, had been a hard blow to the head. She'd been brought into the emergency room unconscious. After several hours of consultation among the doctors, she'd been wheeled into the operating room for a second time, and an operation had been performed to relieve the pressure caused by the hematoma that had resulted from the impact. The operation had gone reasonably well, but the patient had remained in a coma. Now for the first time in five days she was regaining consciousness, and Janie watched anxiously for any signs of brain damage.

Blinking slowly, Rebecca tried to clear her drug-fogged mind and concentrate on what the woman standing above her was saying. Then as full consciousness came, the remembered sound of metal smashing into metal brought a strangled scream from her parched throat. Her head swam dizzily and she had to fight to remain awake.

"Drink a little of this water," Janie encouraged, wishing the doctor would arrive soon.

The cool liquid helped to relieve the discomfort in Rebecca's mouth. Suddenly the remembered sound of a child calling out to her filled her with terror. "Michael...my baby. How badly was he hurt?" she demanded in a raspy whisper.

Janie breathed a sigh of relief. At least the woman had her memory and sounded coherent. "He was a little shook up but he's fine. The safety seat plus the fact that he was in the back seat saved him from any serious injury. According to a witness, you managed to swerve just enough so that you took the brunt of the collision."

"I want to see him." Despite her grogginess, Rebecca managed to look determined. She had heard too many stories of doctors and nurses lying to accident victims about the extent of injuries to family members involved in the same accident. Until she saw her child for herself, she would not believe he was safe.

"Your aunt and uncle took him home several days ago." Janie's tone was apologetic. Anxiously she glanced toward the door. Why wasn't the doctor here when she needed him? It wasn't good for the patient to become agitated.

"I want to see him," Rebecca demanded again.

"The doctor will be here soon. I'm sure he can make some arrangements for that," Janie soothed.

"I have to see my baby." The words came out in a low, pleading moan as Rebecca slid back into the black abyss.

The next time she regained consciousness, she was greeted by her aunt and uncle. Susan and Jack Jacobson had taken her in when her parents had died in a boating accident. Rebecca had been ten at the time. They were an older couple with no children of their own and had welcomed her with an abundance of love and understanding. Even when she had disappointed them by getting pregnant out of wedlock, they had not rejected her nor been judgmental. Instead, they had given her all the support anyone could have wanted, and they loved Michael as if he were their own.

"It's good to see you awake." Susan touched Rebecca's cheek caressingly.

"Michael...how is Michael?" Rebecca asked, staring hard into her aunt's face, attempting to read the truth.

"He's fine. The doctor wouldn't let us bring him

in, but I took a few pictures so you could see for yourself that he's all right.'' The older woman's hands shook slightly as she held the photographs where her niece could view them.

The sight of the two-year-old splashing around in his little rubber swimming pool in the backyard of Susan's home brought a smile to Rebecca's face. ''Thank you,'' she murmured.

''I think Miss Worthen should rest now.'' A nurse, not the one Rebecca remembered from the last time she'd been conscious, approached the bed.

''No, please let them stay,'' Rebecca demanded with all the strength she could muster.

''You're still in intensive care,'' the woman in white explained calmly. ''You need your rest. The doctor only gave permission for your aunt and uncle to come in for a couple of moments to reassure you about your son.''

Rebecca had never been one to turn away from the truth. She knew she was in very serious condition. ''He let them come in because he's not certain I'll live, isn't that so?'' she challenged. The nurse's hesitation was all the confirmation she needed. There were things she had to take care of for Michael's sake.

''You need your rest.'' The woman's voice was

noncommittal as she began to usher the elderly couple out of the room.

"No, wait!" Rebecca's hand tightened on the bed railing. Despite the nearly unbearable pain it caused, she tried to lift herself up into a sitting position.

"Miss Worthen!" The nurse raced back to the bed. "You mustn't strain yourself."

Pain and weakness forcing her to give up the attempt, Rebecca sank back onto her pillow. "Please." Her plea was laced with panic. "I have to speak to my aunt and uncle. It's important." Susan and Jack were in their early sixties. It would be unfair to thrust the burden of raising a child on them at this stage in their lives. Not only that, there were financial considerations. Susan was a retired schoolteacher. Jack was the manager of the local grain-and-feed store in Idaho Falls, Idaho. They had enough money saved for a comfortable retirement. And Rebecca did have some insurance. Still, raising Michael would be a strain on their budget. "Please, I have to talk to them," she insisted, her hands tightening on the bed rails as she prepared herself for another attempt at sitting up.

The nurse noticed the movement and fear for her patient showed in her eyes. "Wait," she ordered Rebecca. For a moment she looked uncertain, then glancing over her shoulder, she nodded for Jack and Susan to reapproach the bed. "No more than five minutes," she stipulated.

"You really should rest," Susan said, watching Rebecca worriedly. "Whatever is on your mind can wait until you're stronger."

"No, it can't wait." Rebecca reached out for Susan's hand and held it for support. She glanced beyond her aunt and uncle. "What I have to say is private. Could we ask the nurse to leave?"

"I'll monitor through the window," the nurse said with an understanding nod.

"I hate asking you to do this," Rebecca began apologetically, looking up into her uncle's face. "It's something I should have taken care of myself. I just didn't know how. I chose to raise Michael on my own. I knew that one day he would ask about his father and I'd have to face confronting Tanner. But I never thought this would happen."

"Now, don't you worry about Michael," Susan said reassuringly. "We'll take care of him. You just spend your energy getting better. Then we'll worry about your confronting this Tanner person."

Rebecca frowned impatiently. "We all know I may not get better." Then she hesitated. Maybe she was misjudging her condition. She turned to her uncle. He'd never been able to hide the truth from her. "Do you think I'm going to get better, Uncle Jack?"

"Of course you're going to recover." Jack's voice was firm. "You're much too young to be taken from us." But Rebecca saw the doubt in his eyes.

Rebecca's jaw firmed. "I have to get my house in order just in case." Her gaze leveled on her uncle. "I need to ask you a favor. A very big favor. A very difficult favor."

Jack's hand closed around his niece's. "You know I'd do anything for you."

"This is going to require some finesse," she cautioned. Mentally she berated herself for not taking care of this sooner. A fog suddenly threatened to cloud her mind. Afraid she would slip back into unconsciousness before she could finish, Rebecca hurried on. "Both of you have been wonderful to me about Michael. You never questioned me about what had happened, how I got pregnant or by whom. You accepted him and me with no restrictions on your love."

Susan gently caressed Rebecca's bruised cheek. "Love knows no restrictions."

"You're wonderful people, and Michael couldn't have anyone better than you to look after him," Rebecca continued. "But I cannot in good conscience place the burden of raising him entirely on your shoulders. The envelope I had Uncle Jack place in his safe contains Michael's father's name. I'm too tired now to tell you the story, but what happened wasn't his fault. We both share equal responsibility. And I know he cares strongly about family.''

''When he didn't marry you, he gave up any claim to the child.'' Jack's voice was strong with emotion.

''Please, don't judge him.'' Rebecca's jaw tensed. ''He never knew I was pregnant.''

Susan looked stunned, as if this possibility had never occurred to her. ''Why didn't you tell him? Was he married?''

''No, not at the time, though he could be now. I don't want to cause him any trouble, but I can't stop thinking that Tanner should be told about his son. This is a delicate matter, and I'm counting on your judgment and tact, Uncle Jack. Please be discreet...'' The words trailed off as Rebecca again drifted into unconsciousness.

Tanner stood by the corral watching the Cessna approach. He was a big man, tall, with muscles strengthened and toned by a lifetime of working with horses and cattle. As the plane neared, he removed the dusty tan Stetson he was wearing and wiped the perspiration from his brow with the sleeve of his shirt. Agitatedly, he used his fingers to comb the sweat-matted, thick black hair from his face. There was nothing soft about the rancher's features. The cheekbones were high, the jaw square. The nose was average in size with a slight bump just below the bridge giving evidence that it had once been broken. There was a sensuality about the mouth when he smiled, but at the moment his expression conveyed no amusement. Instead, there was a coldness in the steel-blue depths of his eyes as he watched the plane land. Starting toward the house, he again wondered what a stranger from Idaho Falls, Idaho, would have to talk to him about. Especially something that was so private it couldn't be discussed on the phone and so urgent the man had insisted on their meeting as quickly as possible.

As the plane circled once before landing, Jack peered out of the window of the Cessna at the huge, sprawling ranch house flanked by numerous corrals and outbuildings. The Cessna belonged to Tanner Lathrop, and the pilot was Jim Gordon, Lathrop's foreman. Lathrop had sent Gordon to pick up Jack in San Angelo for the final leg of the journey to this desolate region of west Texas. Through casual conversation, Jack had learned that Tanner Lathrop was not married, nor had he ever been. "Ain't no woman been able to corral him yet," Jim had said with an amused gleam in his eyes, as if he doubted any woman ever would.

Jack managed to force a smile as bile rose in his throat. He'd almost told the pilot to take him back to San Angelo then and there, but he'd made Rebecca a promise.

The extent of Lathrop's wealth had come as a surprise. During the flight, Jim Gordon had pointed out where the Lathrop spread began. That had been some time ago. Since then, they'd flown over a field of oil derricks, all of which had been pumping.

Jack scowled. It was the character of the people who raised a child that was important, not their wealth. And he had grave doubts about Tanner Lathrop's character. Rebecca was a sweet, loving, decent woman, the kind any man should have been proud to have as a wife. But instead, the Texan had bedded her and then walked away without a backward glance. Even though Rebecca was insistent that what had happened between her and Lathrop had not been the rancher's fault, Jack knew how difficult her life had been because of it. As far as he was concerned, Tanner Lathrop had a great deal to answer for.

"Thought I'd circle once to give you a bird's-eye view," Jim Gordon said in an easy drawl as he completed the landing and turned off the engine.

Jack glanced toward him. He wasn't fooled. He knew they had circled the ranch house to give Tanner plenty of warning of their arrival. But he didn't care how much warning the man had. He felt like a knight going into battle. For Rebecca, he would face the devil himself.

"Sorry I couldn't meet you in San Angelo," Tanner said, extending his hand in greeting. "But I had pressing business here at the ranch."

Jack was fairly certain that was a lie. As a businessman, he'd played this game many times. Lathrop had wanted to meet at the ranch because he felt he had an advantage here.

Certainly the house itself was impressive. It was large and tastefully furnished with leather-upholstered chairs and couches and highly polished fine wood tables. The desk in Lathrop's study was a massive, roughly hewn oak affair. On the opposite wall was a painting by Remington. Handwoven Indian rugs, hung on other walls. Without being ostentatious, the place had an air of wealth and power. Then there was the sense of isolation, the thought that for miles around there was nothing but Lathrop land.

And, of course, there was Tanner Lathrop himself. Dressed in his faded jeans, work shirt and scuffed boots, he was the epitome of every child's idea of a real cowboy. The steadfast and true western hero that could easily turn a young girl's head, Jack mused cynically. He, however, was not taken in by the image, nor was he intimidated by the man's wealth.

"I appreciate you seeing me on such short notice," Jack said, accepting the handshake. The feel of callus on the rancher's hand surprised him. Tanner Lathrop obviously was no Sunday cowboy. But that didn't make him a hero, either.

As he rounded his desk and seated himself, Tanner waved a hand toward one of the comfortable-looking leather-upholstered chairs as an invitation for Jack to be seated. "And now that we're meeting face-to-face as you insisted," he said, "what is it you've come to discuss?"

Jack had spent hours practicing various avenues of approach. But suddenly he was at a loss as to how to proceed. For Rebecca's sake he'd tried to fight the prejudice he felt toward this man, but it was a losing battle. All he could see was his niece being taken advantage of by this Texan.

Tanner Lathrop scowled impatiently. "I'm a busy man, Mr. Jacobson. I've got a ranch to run. So if you don't mind, I'd appreciate it if you'd state your business."

Jack knew how much Rebecca loved her son. She wouldn't consider leaving him at the mercy of someone she didn't think would treat him well. However, Jack's doubts about the man were growing stronger with each passing moment. Rebecca had told him to use his judgment and tact, and he'd do just that. Choosing to feel Tanner out before revealing too much, Jack schooled his features into an expression of cool detachment. "Mr. Lathrop, do you recall knowing a young woman by the name of Rebecca Worthen?"

A coldness entered the rancher's eyes. "Maybe I do and maybe I don't. Describe her."

Jack's hands balled into white-knuckled fists as he fought to maintain a neutral expression on his face. The man wanted a description as if Rebecca were a cheap call girl he had to pick out of a lineup. Jack didn't care that he was making a decision based on emotion rather than reason. All he knew was that, in his opinion, Michael was better off never meeting this man. He rose to his feet.

"I don't believe there's any reason to proceed any further with this conversation," he said with finality. "If you will arrange for me to be flown back to San Angelo, I won't waste any more of your time."

Jack started toward the door, but the rancher moved faster. Before Jack could make his exit, he was blocked by the Texan. "You came a long way to ask one question and then leave," Tanner observed dryly.

Jack's shoulders squared. "Your answer told me all I needed to know." A liturgy of recriminations he would liked to have delivered played through his mind, but he held his tongue. He was determined to protect Michael and Rebecca from this cowboy.

Tanner's jaw flexed slightly as if he was having trouble keeping his temper under control. The coldness in his eyes turned to ice. "Mr. Jacobson, I've had the feeling you've been passing judgment on me ever since you got here. I insist on knowing what this is all about."

Jack met the man's demand with equal resolve. "You can insist all you like. I have nothing more to say to you."

Tanner continued to block the door. "I want to know why you're asking questions about Rebecca Worthen."

One corner of Jack's mouth tilted sarcastically.

"Surely a woman you cannot recall without a description could not be of any real interest to you."

Tanner shrugged, a cool indifference descending over his features. "I simply wanted to be certain we were talking about the same Rebecca Worthen. The one I knew lived in Philadelphia. Idaho's a long way from there."

The slim hold Jack had on his control snapped. "Obviously we're not talking about the same woman," he snarled. "I can't imagine the Rebecca I know being involved with the likes of you."

Anger replaced the indifference in the cowboy's eyes. "And exactly what do you mean by that?"

Jack took a deep breath. He'd almost said too much. "Never mind. I was out of line. Would you please arrange for me to be taken back to the airport?"

But Tanner didn't move. Instead, he continued to study the man in front of him. "I'd say you stepped very far out of line."

"I apologize if I offended your sensitivities." Jack tried to keep his tone neutral but instead, it had an underlying flavor that suggested he doubted the cowboy had any sensitivities.

Tanner's gaze narrowed warningly. "I want to know why you came to see me and what your connection to Rebecca is. If I have to hire private detectives to watch you twenty-four hours a day, I'll do it.''

The cold steel in the Texan's eyes was proof to Jack that this was no idle threat. He walked back toward the center of the room, giving himself a chance to think. If Tanner Lathrop had him followed, the rancher was certain to find out about Michael. He might put two and two together and figure out that he was the boy's father, and right now that was the last thing in the world Jack wanted to happen. He had to talk to Rebecca again. He had to make her see that this man should not be allowed to have Michael—at least, not without restrictions. Wishing he was not so emotionally involved, he tried to come up with an explanation that wasn't a lie but would keep the cowboy from investigating. ''Rebecca is my niece,'' he began slowly.

''And she sent you here to see if I remember her?'' Tanner interjected with cynical amusement, as if he found Rebecca's renewed interest in him humorous.

Jack struggled to keep his temper in check. ''I came of my own accord,'' he replied coolly. This wasn't entirely a lie. Rebecca had not requested that he travel to Texas to interview the man personally. But he cared too much for Michael to reveal the boy's existence to Tanner without first meeting the man face-to-face.

The amusement was gone as Tanner once again studied his visitor. "That brings us back to my original question. Why did you come?"

The cowboy was persistent, Jack fumed. "I had my reasons, but they're of no concern to you," he replied firmly.

Tanner's jaw hardened with resolve. "Apparently I'll have to contact Rebecca to get to the bottom of this."

"No!" The word came out with vehement command. "You stay away from Idaho Falls and away from her."

For a long moment Tanner regarded the older man in silence, then he said levelly, "This interview is making less and less sense by the minute. Whether you like it or not, I intend to find out what's behind your visit."

Jack's only concern now was to protect Rebecca. The thought of this man intruding on her last days made him ill. "As we speak, Rebecca is lying in the hospital very likely dying, Mr. Lathrop. I won't allow you to harass her."

Tanner flinched as if he'd received a physical blow, and for a moment Jack wondered if he'd misjudged him. Then the coldness returned to the

Texan's eyes. "If what you say is true, it would appear to be a little late for her to have decided she wants a reconciliation."

The cynical edge in the rancher's voice, as if he found the thought of reconciliation with Rebecca absurd, was the final straw. "Rebecca is not interested in seeing you. My coming here was a mistake and I apologize for having taken up your time," Jack seethed. "Now, will you please arrange for my transportation back to San Angelo?"

Again Tanner ignored the request. Impatience etched itself into his features. "It would appear we're back to square one. Why did you come?"

Jack had never been good at lying. He settled for a darkly shaded truth. "During a period of delirium, Rebecca mentioned your name and where you could be found. I thought perhaps you were a special friend of hers, but that is obviously not the case. Therefore, I would appreciate it if you would arrange for me to leave. And I think it would be best for everyone if we both forget this visit ever happened."

For a brief moment, Tanner continued to regard his guest in silence. Then, giving a shrug, he strode to the phone and made the necessary arrangements for Jack to leave.

As he was being driven back to the landing strip,

Jack breathed a sigh of relief. Tanner had said nothing more about Rebecca, and Jack accepted the man's silence on the matter as an agreement to forget it. Climbing into the Cessna, he began forming his arguments to present to Rebecca. He and Susan were getting on in years, but they loved Michael, and they would give him a good home. Besides, he wasn't ready to believe that Rebecca was going to die.

Tanner stood looking out his study window as the plane took off. When it was in the air, he turned away abruptly and strode to his desk. Picking up the phone, he dialed a number. "Hello, Joe. Tanner here. I need to make a few phone calls to determine my destination. Then I'd like to borrow your pilot and that fancy jet of yours for a trip."

Chapter Two

Rebecca lay with her eyes closed. Her mind was groggy but she was conscious. The doctors had allowed Susan to bring Michael in to see her. The visit had lasted only a few minutes, but it had assured her that he was all right. Now she lay trying to hold his image in her mind. It gave her the will to fight for life.

But Michael's image kept fading into another image—the image of a man with the same black hair and blue eyes as her son. The resemblance between Michael and Tanner was strong. There were moments, especially when Michael was being difficult, she'd look at him and he'd have his jaw set in a determined line that made him look so much like his father. As a general rule, however, she tried never to think about Tanner. But today that was proving impossible. Susan had told her that Jack had flown out to Tanner's ranch.

"Your uncle thought it would be wise to meet the man. Then he'll decide how and what to tell him about Michael," Susan had explained.

Meet the man. The words echoed in Rebecca's head. She'd been certain the memories of Tanner would fade through the years, but they hadn't. She could still recall the first time she saw him as clearly as if it had happened yesterday....

It was the winter of her second year after college. Determined to pay off her school debts as quickly as possible and save some money on the side, she was working at two jobs. During the day she had a position as an accountant in the credit department of a large department store in Philadelphia. At night she worked as a waitress in Cactus Anne's, a club that catered to the country-and-western crowd. The food was passable. The patrons came mostly to drink and listen and dance to the music provided by local talent.

In keeping with the western motif, the waitresses were required to wear jeans, shirts and cowboy boots. After having put in a long day wearing a suit and high-heeled shoes, Rebecca was grateful for the comfortable uniform. When she got home from her day job, she'd quickly change, braid her long brunette hair into a single pigtail at the back of her neck, apply a touch of fresh makeup and she was ready.

Tanner had been brought to Cactus Anne's by Frank Henderson, a native Philadelphian and one of the regulars. Normally Rebecca was not aware of new arrivals, but when Tanner entered, there had been a rash of whispering among several of the single females present. Curiosity had caused her to glance toward the door. He had an imposing presence. Covertly, she let her gaze travel from his Stetson hat to the tailored business suit and string tie, then downward to the expensive, hand-tooled-leather boots. Cynically, she classified him as an urban cowboy. But she'd been wrong about that.

"Tanner here is a real Texas cowboy," Frank had informed her when she'd approached their table to take their order. "I brought him to Cactus Anne's so he could tell me just how authentic the 'Texas chili' is."

"It's as authentic as our Italian cook can make it," she quipped. This was a line she'd repeated a hundred times before. It came out automatically. She barely noticed she'd said anything as she found herself looking into a pair of the bluest eyes she'd ever seen.

Frank laughed. "Tanner Lathrop, meet Rebecca," he said jovially. "Rebecca, this is Tanner Lathrop. He's in town on business for a couple of weeks."

"Rebecca." Tanner removed his hat in acknowledgment of the introduction. He smiled politely as he repeated her name, but the smile didn't reach his eyes. Instead, they regarded her speculatively.

Rebecca had seen that look before. He was wondering how available she was. Well, she wasn't available at all. Her expression became cool and distant. "I hope you have a nice stay," she replied with formal courtesy, then asked, "Are you gentlemen ready to order now, or would you like something from the bar first?"

"I'll have a beer," Frank replied, giving Tanner a warning glance.

"Same here," Tanner added.

As she turned to leave, Rebecca heard Frank saying in a lowered voice, "Rebecca's a cold one. It's Kathy I was hoping to introduce you to, but it looks as if she's not here tonight. We can leave if you'd like."

Rebecca knew Kathy liked to party. Obviously Frank was attempting to find a companion for Tanner who would make his stay in Philadelphia entertaining. The thought irritated her. Surprised she'd had any reaction, she shrugged to discard it. Mentally she placed a wager with herself that they'd ask for their bill and leave as soon as she returned with their beer. And that'd be just fine with her, she affirmed.

"Think I'll try that Texas chili," Tanner said as she placed his beer in front of him.

She glanced toward him to find him studying her again. Working here, she'd had a lot of men give her the once-over. She knew she wasn't beautiful. She was average, pleasant to look at, but not the kind to turn men's heads when she walked by. Usually her cold-shoulder routine caused them to lose interest immediately. But not only was this Texan showing continued interest, she was finding herself curiously affected by it. She felt both unnerved and excited at the same time.

Concentrate on his order, she commanded herself. Aloud, she said lightly, "It's your stomach," jotted down his order, then turned her attention to Frank. "And what can I get for you?" she asked, trying to ignore the prickling on the side of her neck that told her Tanner was still watching her.

"I'll settle for the steak and a salad," Frank responded, an amused gleam in his eyes.

"I'll have that, too, in addition to the chili," Tanner said.

Rebecca didn't look at him. She merely nodded to let him know she'd heard. It was cowardly, but the strength of her awareness of him frightened her a little.

As she moved away, she heard Frank saying, "If I'd known you were a man who liked challenges, there's this blonde, a real knock-out..." There was a strong suggestive edge to his words that implied he thought they should go seeking this new conquest.

"I prefer to choose my own challenges," Tanner replied in an easy drawl.

The muscles in Rebecca's back stiffened. A challenge! So that was how he saw her. Well, he was going to discover he was wasting his time. She didn't play games and she didn't like men who did.

Anger built a wall of cool reserve around her. The prickling sensation on her neck no longer unnerved her. Mr. Lathrop could watch her all he wanted. The only thing his gaze caused now was irritation.

When she served them their food, she barely gave him a glance. Out of the corner of her eye she saw Frank giving him a look that said, *I warned you that you were wasting your time.*

What did surprise her was Tanner's behavior. She'd expected him to make a pass, which she planned to meet with icy rebuff. But instead, he treated her with polite respect—thanking her when she placed the food in front of him and not making any suggestive comments or even flirting mildly.

Obviously he'd lost all interest in this "challenge," she mused dryly as she walked away from the table. Recalling the sensation of being unexpectedly captivated by those blue eyes of his, she guessed he normally had no trouble making conquests. And despite what he'd told Frank, he clearly preferred women who fell easily. He'll probably gulp down his food and leave, she concluded.

Again, she guessed wrongly about Mr. Tanner Lathrop. He ate leisurely, periodically watching the band and the dancers.

Not that I'm interested in what he does, she told herself. Besides, she had an even bigger nuisance to watch out for than the Texas cowboy. A group of five boisterous men in their mid-twenties had come in. They seated themselves at the table next to the cowboy's.

"Thought we'd have a few drinks and listen to the band," the big blonde who seemed to be in command of the group announced with a wide grin when she approached. "We keep hearing about how this country-and-western music is the new thing.''

The slight slurring of his speech told her that he'd already had a few drinks, and from the snickers and guffaws that issued from the rest, she guessed they had, too. She'd seen their kind before. They came in, made whispered derogatory remarks among themselves about the music and customers, then left feeling superior. Taking their order for beer all round, she hoped they'd get bored and leave quickly. If they stayed, there was always the potential for trouble, especially if they got even drunker and began making their comments loud enough to annoy the other patrons.

''You fill those jeans out real nice, babe,'' the blonde called after her as she walked away.

She'd heard such remarks before and had learned to take no notice. But at the moment she wasn't feeling very tolerant. Tanner Lathrop had already unsettled her. She'd never lost her temper with a customer before, but tonight she was having a difficult time holding on to her control. ''They'd better leave soon or I won't be responsible for my actions,'' she muttered under her breath, continuing toward the bar without a backward glance.

Returning with their beer, she placed the drinks on the table. Straightening, she poised her pencil above the order pad and asked, "Is there anything else I can get for you gentlemen?"

"Well, now…" The blonde's voice took on a lecherous quality. He reached out to pat her on the seat.

Rebecca tensed. *If he touches me, he'll regret it,* she promised herself.

But before the contact could be made, Tanner leaned back in his chair and caught the man's wrist. "I wouldn't do that if I were you," he warned.

A belligerent expression spread over the big blonde's face. Attempting to jerk free, he growled, "I'll do—"

Tanner interrupted him. "She looks a bit riled, and it's been my experience that an angry woman can be a hell of a lot more dangerous than ten men." He'd tightened his grip on the man's wrist, and his eyes held a warning, but there was an edge of amusement in his voice that gave the other man an out.

The blonde took it. "You're right," he said, a comradely grin replacing the anger on his face.

Rebecca watched as Tanner released his hold and returned his attention to his dinner. She'd never seen a man who could act so friendly yet be so intimidating at the same time. Turning her attention to the blonde, she noticed that he looked visibly shaken.

The others at the table sat mutely, watching their leader as if uncertain of what to expect.

"This place bores me," the blonde abruptly announced loudly. "Drink up and let's get out of here. I want to find a place where people know how to have fun." Without taking the time to pour his beer from the bottle into the glass, he downed it in one long swallow.

"Yeah," the others chorused. Picking up their bottles, they all followed his example, slamming the bottles down on the table when they finished. Like children who have to be the center of attention, Rebecca thought, as they tossed money on the table to cover their drinks, then sauntered out.

She was starting to clear the table when a male voice said in what was beginning to be a very familiar drawl, "You might thank me." She turned to tell him that she could have taken care of the situation herself. But before she could speak, he added, "I figure I saved you your job and from being charged with assault. You looked as if you were ready to take on that whole bunch single-handed. And it's my guess you would have won."

He was grinning at her, and the laughter in his eyes was contagious. In spite of herself, she smiled.

"You could be right," she heard herself replying. Quickly she returned her attention to clearing the table. That cowboy was dangerous. Even knowing that he saw her only as a challenge, she was feeling an attraction for him. *I've definitely been working too many hours,* she told herself.

In the kitchen, she arranged to switch tables with Beth. It was a bit cowardly, but the cowboy made her uneasy, and it had always been her philosophy to avoid trouble when possible.

"And he was definitely trouble," she muttered under her breath when he left a while later. While he was there, she'd tried hard to ignore his presence, but it had been futile. She'd not only found herself covertly watching him, she'd felt annoyed when several of the single-women customers had tried to get him to dance.

She breathed a sign of relief. Now that he was gone she could put him out of her mind. Curiously, however, although the place was now packed and there was a line of customers at the door waiting to get in, it felt strangely empty. *I've got to take some time off,* she told herself curtly. *Go out on a few dates. Clearly, I'm suffering from a deprivation of male companionship.*

But it wasn't just any male's company that continued to nag at her for the rest of the evening. It was the cowboy's image that kept coming back into her mind.

Finally it was time to go home. *He's gone and you're never going to see him again, so just forget about him,* she told herself as she walked outside. She was tired, and the only thing she wanted to think about was crawling into bed and getting a few hours' sleep.

"Thought I'd stick around and make certain no more customers needed me to rescue them. It occurred to me that some fool might try to walk you to your car."

Rebecca swung around to find Tanner leaning casually against the wall of the building. Her heart began pounding double time. *Keep in mind why he's here,* she ordered herself. *You're a challenge to him. Nothing more.* "That was really unnecessary," she said stiffly.

Straightening, he began moving toward her. "Truth is, I was wondering if I could buy you coffee or a late dinner."

The urge to say yes was strong. *He's just determined to prove he can win over any woman,* she warned herself. "No thanks," she replied coolly. He was near her now. She'd seen handsomer men, but none of them had ever looked this good to her before. Abruptly, she turned away and started toward her car.

Tanner fell into step beside her. "Look, I know we got off to a bad start…"

The attraction she was feeling both scared and angered her. Coming to a halt, she again faced him. "We never got off to any start," she corrected frostily. Her back stiffened. "I am not a 'challenge,' Mr. Lathrop. And I don't like men who think of women in those terms."

His jaw tensed. "I thought that might be the problem." A coaxing quality entered his voice. "I didn't mean that the way it sounded. How about giving me a second chance?"

Again the urge to say yes was almost overwhelming. But he was only in town on business, she reminded herself. He'd be gone in a couple of weeks. And she wasn't interested in short-term romances. "I don't think so," she replied with finality, then continued on to her car.

But as she started the engine, she couldn't stop herself from glancing back at him. He was walking toward the entrance of Cactus Anne's. He wouldn't get in—the place was closed. Her gaze traveled around the parking lot. She recognized the few remaining cars as belonging to other employees.

After backing out, she glanced back at him again.

He was walking toward the street. The weather wasn't bad and she did need to get home and get some sleep, but she couldn't make herself leave him there. He didn't know this town, and this wasn't the best place to be stranded in the small hours of the night.

She pulled up beside him and rolled down the window.

"You wouldn't happen to know where there's a phone booth so I can call a cab," he asked.

"I do," she replied, "but it'll take a while before a cab can get here. I'll give you a lift to your hotel if you like." She couldn't believe she hadn't just offered to take him to a phone booth. Well, he *had* saved her from an embarrassing situation. She owed him some kindness, she reasoned.

"I was under the impression you found my company about as appealing as a rattlesnake's," he said as he opened the door and slid into the passenger's seat.

"I figure I owe you," she replied coolly, not wanting him to think this was anything more than her paying back a debt. Close proximity to him was causing a weakening of her resolve. If he asked her out again, she might accept.

A matching coolness descended over his features as he gave her the name of his hotel. "If it's too far out of your way, you can just drop me off at a phone booth.''

His tone let her know he'd given up trying to date her. She should have felt relieved, but instead a wave of disappointment swept through her. *I just need to get some rest,* she assured herself. The hotel was out of her way and she considered dropping him off at one of the quick-stop stores that was open all night. They always had phones right outside and he could wait inside until his cab arrived. But instead, she heard herself saying, ''It's practically on my way.''

Neither talked as she drove. To her relief, the traffic was sparse and she hit mostly green lights. When she pulled up in front of his hotel, he thanked her politely, then walked away.

''And that's the end of Mr. Tanner Lathrop,'' she declared as she pulled out onto the street.

But that night the blue-eyed Texan haunted her dreams, and the next morning she awoke feeling restless.

Forget him, she ordered herself as she drove to work. But several times during the day, the rows of numbers on her computer blurred and his image came sharply back. By five o'clock she was ready to admit that no other man had ever affected her so strongly.

You'll never be seeing him again, so you may as well put him out of your mind, she told herself for the umpteenth time as she entered her apartment and kicked off her shoes.

Tonight was her night off. "Laundry night," she announced to the emptiness around her. Normally she followed this statement with a groan, but tonight she was almost glad of the diversion. The restlessness with which she had awoken still lingered. Usually she enjoyed an evening of solitude. But tonight, sitting quietly around her apartment just reading or watching television seemed particularly unappealing.

Too tense to eat, she changed into a pair of old shorts and a shirt. Ten minutes later she was shoving her dirty laundry into two of the washing machines housed in the basement of her building. It was too early for those who liked to wash in the evening to be coming in, and those who did their laundry during the day had left. She had the room to herself. After starting the machines, she seated herself on the next one in the row and began to read the newspaper.

A boring hour and a half later, the laundry was finished. "My life could use a little excitement," she informed the button board of the elevator as she punched in the number of her floor. Again the im-

age of the cowboy came into her mind. "Something
a little less dangerous than him," she specified.
Then she frowned at herself. He was merely a man.
The only thing dangerous about him was the effect
he was having on her. She couldn't get him out of
her mind.

The elevator door opened and she blinked. It had
to be a hallucination. She could swear she saw Tanner Lathrop leaning on the wall next to the door of
her apartment. He was dressed in a gray suit. His
booted feet were crossed at the ankles. His hands
were shoved into the pockets of his slacks, and his
Stetson was tilted down over his eyes as if he were
napping.

Chapter Three

Stepping out of the elevator, she blinked again. He was still there. She grimaced as a rivulet of sweat ran down her cheek and dripped off. *One look at me like this should send him running,* she thought. The laundry room had been like a sauna. Her shirt and shorts were sweat-soaked and clinging. Her hair hung in long damp strands down her back. Most of her makeup was on a towel she'd used to wipe the perspiration from her face. Fortunately she'd worn only a light amount of mascara and it was the waterproof type, so her eyes didn't have black smudges under them.

As if he suddenly felt her watching him, Tanner

straightened, tilted his hat back and turned toward her. "Evening," he said politely. The hint of a relieved grin played at one corner of his mouth. "I was beginning to be afraid you'd gone out on a date for the evening and I was going to become rooted to this spot before you got back."

Rebecca was still having a difficult time believing he was actually there. "How did you find me?" she asked in a stunned voice.

Instead of answering, he nodded toward the door of her apartment. "Your phone's ringing."

Reacting automatically, she jogged to the door. Still holding the duffel bag of clean laundry, box of detergent and bottle of fabric softener, she managed to unlock the door. As she entered the apartment, her answering machine was finishing its appeal for the caller to leave a message.

"Hi, Rebecca, this is Kathy," said a voice as soon as the beep had sounded. "Don't be angry with me. I gave that Texan your address. He came by tonight and was asking about you. I'd already told him about you working at Wanamaker's during the day, so I figured he could find you, anyway. And Frank vouched for him—said he was a millionaire oilman. That must be true. He gave me a hundred dollars for the information. Anyway, fifty of it is yours if you won't be angry. Thought I'd call and warn you. See you Saturday.''

Rebecca swung around to find Tanner standing in the open doorway of her apartment. ''You paid Kathy a hundred dollars for my address?'' she demanded in a voice filled with suspicion.

He removed his hat and a look of mild embarrassment spread over his features. ''I hadn't intended to make a nuisance of myself. But all day I couldn't get you out of my mind.'' He gave his head a small shake as he couldn't quite believe this himself. ''I've never had this kind of reaction to a female before. I just wanted to see you again.''

Rebecca knew exactly what he was talking about. Considering her appearance, however, she guessed he was now cured of his need to see her.

But Tanner didn't show any signs of leaving. Instead, he asked, ''Would you mind if I come in?''

''I guess not,'' she replied, then scowled at the uncertainty in her voice. She was used to being more in control. But at the moment she felt like a schoolgirl. *Get a grip on yourself,* she ordered.

Tanner stepped inside and closed the door.

To Rebecca, the room seemed to shrink to about the size of a matchbox.

''I was wondering if you'd go out to dinner with me,'' he said.

Her heart was racing. The attraction she felt for him was almost like a physical force. She'd heard about animal magnetism before, but she'd never believed in it. The safe thing to do would be to refuse and send him on his way, her inner voice cautioned, but instead, she heard herself saying apologetically, "It'll take me a while to get ready."

He smiled. It softened his features and her heart pounded even harder. "I don't mind waiting," he replied, moving toward the sofa.

"All right," she managed. Just looking at him caused a thrill of pleasure that made her reluctant to move. *Any moment now you're going to start drooling,* she admonished herself. Ordering her legs to move, she grabbed her clean laundry, then went into the bedroom. As she set the duffel bag down, she noticed that her hands were shaking. "I'm behaving like an adolescent on my first date," she muttered.

She had a stern talk with herself all the time she was taking her shower, fixing her hair and dressing. By the time she was ready to return to the living room, she was certain she had her emotions under control.

"You look very nice," he said, rising from the couch to greet her.

His gaze seemed to touch her physically. And the

expression of pleasure on his face caused her legs to feel strangely weak and her heart to lurch. So much for control, she mused dryly. The temptation to say he looked very nice, too, was strong, but she settled for a polite thank-you.

She had to force herself to concentrate on what he was saying as he told her about the dinner reservation he'd made. She kept finding herself watching his lips and wondering what they would feel like on hers....

"Frank suggested the place. I'll drive, but you'll have to direct me." He smiled quirkily. "This time, I've rented a car. I didn't want to end up stranded in case you refused to have anything to do with me."

All she could manage was a nod. She hoped she didn't get them lost. At the moment, she wasn't certain she could direct anyone to her local grocery.

She did, however, get them there without mishap. It was one of the more expensive restaurants in town. She'd planned on ordering only a minimum of food, but he insisted that she order an item from each course.

"Eating our way through all the courses should give us some time to get to know one another better," he said as the waiter left.

And it did. By the time they'd finished dessert,

she knew a great deal about his family's ranch in Texas. She knew his father's ancestors had settled the land when it still belonged to Mexico. His father was still living. His mother had died of cancer a couple of years earlier. Tanner was the only child and would one day inherit everything. At the moment, he and his father jointly ran the ranch. "But he's the boss, and everyone knows it," Tanner had finished in a tone that let her know he was very fond of his father and respected him greatly.

As for her, he'd learned that her parents had been killed in a boating accident when she was ten and that she'd been raised by a loving aunt and uncle. But unlike his family, hers wasn't wealthy. They were middle-class, and paying for her college education would have been a burden on her aunt and uncle. They'd insisted on helping with some of the expenses, but she'd worked and borrowed to pay for the major portion. "I wanted to do it myself," she explained. "My aunt says I inherited my stubborn independence from my father—her brother." A look of pride came into her eyes. "And in one more year I'll have paid off my debts."

He was smiling at her. "I'm glad I came looking for you."

"I'm glad, too," she admitted.

As they drove back to her apartment, she rattled

on about the various bands who came to play at Cactus Anne's. She knew she must sound inane, but whenever she let her mind wander freely, she came back to wondering what it would feel like to be in his arms. He lived more than halfway across the country and he was going back home in only a few days, she kept reminding herself. She'd likely never see him again. Until now she'd never had any trouble maintaining control over her emotions where men were concerned. She knew what she wanted— a home and family. She didn't want an affair, and she especially wasn't interested in a one-night stand. But no man had ever made her feel this way. Just being near Tanner caused a heated excitement in the pit of her stomach.

As they rode up in the elevator to her apartment, the urge to ask him in for a cup of coffee was strong, but her instincts warned her against it. For the first time in her life, she didn't trust herself to behave rationally.

"Can I see you tomorrow?" he asked when they reached her door.

She wanted to say yes, but there were practical concerns she couldn't ignore. "I have to work," she heard herself saying with regret.

He traced the line of her jaw with the tip of his

fingers. "Call in sick and spend the day with me," he coaxed.

She felt herself being drawn into the warm blue depths of his eyes. The desire to agree to anything he suggested swept over her. *Don't behave like an irrational schoolgirl,* she ordered herself. *It can only lead to trouble.* "I really can't," she forced herself to say.

"That's too bad." Regret was strong in his voice. Cupping her face in his hands, he bent down and kissed her.

It was a light kiss, the kind a person might give a friend. But it sent her blood racing. Even after the contact had been broken, her lips still felt the lingering warmth of his.

Leaving the tips of his fingers still touching her face, he asked, "If I come by Cactus Anne's tomorrow night, will you go out for a late dinner with me?"

If she did that she wouldn't get more than a couple of hours' sleep, she knew. But sleep didn't seem important at the moment. "That sounds nice," she replied.

"Until tomorrow then," he said. As if adding confirmation to their date, he kissed her on the tip of her nose. Then releasing her completely, he stepped back to allow her to unlock her door.

Rebecca wasn't certain how she got the key in the lock. Her arms, her legs, her entire body felt uncoordinated. But she managed to get inside her apartment without looking like a clumsy fool.

Tanner tipped his hat and smiled. "See you tomorrow," he said when she turned back toward him.

"Tomorrow," she replied, then closed the door. But with her hand still on the knob, her breath caught in her lungs as an acute sense of aloneness swept over her. Her apartment suddenly seemed cold and empty. Tanner's image filled her mind. She didn't want him to leave. Without even realizing what she was doing, she jerked open the door.

He hadn't moved. She'd expected him to already be gone, but he was still standing outside her door. "Rebecca?" He spoke in a low, questioning growl.

She couldn't think of anything to reply. Her teeth closed over her bottom lip, and she stepped back from the door in a silent invitation for him to enter....

Later Rebecca lay quietly, her cheek resting on Tanner's shoulder. When she'd heard other women talking about being swept away by what they termed the magic of the moment, she'd assured herself that would never happen to her. But that was before Tanner Lathrop had entered her life. She felt wanton and ashamed of herself for having been so weak. But what was done was done. There was no sense in feeling regret. "I've always wondered if sex was overrated," she heard herself saying. "Now I know it isn't." She flushed at the openness of this statement, then gave a mental shrug. It was the truth.

Levering himself up on an elbow, Tanner looked down at her. "You should have told me you were a virgin."

She read the guilt etched into his features. Her body tensed. What had happened hadn't been his fault. She'd been a consenting adult. One who was caught up in a moment of insanity, she clarified, recalling how his touch had vanquished rational thought. But consenting nonetheless, she added. And she refused to allow him to feel obligated to her just because he was the first man to "know" her fully. Forcing a nonchalance into her voice, she said, "A girl can't stay a virgin forever."

Concern replaced the guilt. Gently, he combed wayward strands of hair back from her face. "I'm sorry if I hurt you."

The softness in his eyes sent a current of warmth through her while his touch caused a tingling of pleasure. Wanton wench! she scolded herself. Then she heard herself admitting honestly, "Pain isn't my most vivid memory of the experience.'' She gave a mental gasp at her continued openness. This wasn't like her at all.

He smiled. ''You are delicious,'' he said as he kissed her lightly. Then tossing off the sheet, he rose from the bed and began to dress.

A hard knot formed in her stomach. She'd expected him to stay the night. Obviously he hadn't enjoyed her company as much as she'd enjoyed his. Her jaw tensed with pride. She'd probably only enjoyed it so much because it was so new, she told herself. It was just as well that he was leaving before she got bored with him.

Still, his quick desertion stung. When he sat down on the edge of the bed to pull on his boots, she had a tremendous urge to literally kick him off. But the determination to maintain her dignity won, and she simply lay quietly waiting for him to make his exit.

Turning back toward her, he leaned down and kissed her. ''I'd stay, but I know I couldn't keep my hands off you and I figure you need some rest.'' Kissing her a final time, he rose and left.

For a long time after he was gone, Rebecca lay quietly. She wanted to believe he hadn't really wanted to leave. But she was a realist. She'd known too many women who had given in to their emotions and in the gray light of dawn found themselves alone.

"It just felt so right," she murmured, still stunned by her wantonness.

The next morning when her alarm went off, she almost called in sick. It had been late when she'd finally dozed off, and she awoke with a headache. But as sharp memories of the night before came flooding back, she dragged herself out of bed. The last thing she wanted to do was lie there, remembering and berating herself for her weakness.

After starting a pot of coffee perking, she went in and showered. The hot water soothed her headache, and she was beginning to feel more like her normal self by the time she'd toweled dry.

She was on her way back to the kitchen when a knock sounded on her door. Glancing at the clock, she frowned. Who in the world would come calling at this hour of the morning? "Probably Joyce," she guessed, picturing the redhead who lived next door. "She's always running out of milk." But Rebecca was not in the mood to see anyone just yet. She decided to ignore the summons when the knock came again.

Giving in to the inevitable, she made sure the belt of her robe was securely fastened, then swung open the door.

But it wasn't Joyce. It was Tanner. He looked tired, as if he hadn't slept at all.

"I've been thinking," he said, entering and closing the door. "You and I should get married."

Chapter Four

"Married?" Rebecca stared at him in disbelief. His expression was shuttered, but the guilt she'd seen in his eyes the night before when he'd discovered she was a virgin came sharply back into her mind. Her shoulders squared with pride. "That really isn't necessary. I'm not a naive child. We were two consenting adults."

He regarded her dryly. "Is that your polite way of saying you're not interested in marrying me?"

"I just don't think it's a good idea to rush into something so important," she replied honestly. Looking at him, the attraction she felt was as strong as ever. The truth was she *did* want to marry him, but she wasn't all that certain he wanted to marry her. "I don't want us to jump into something either one of us will regret. It would be smarter if we took some time to get to know one another better."

"I'd say we know one another very well," he countered.

"In the biblical sense," she replied. "But marriage involves a lot more than sex."

He shrugged. "Offering seemed like the right thing to do."

Her stomach knotted. He'd just admitted that his basic motivation was guilt. And she probably only wanted to marry him because of her basic conservative upbringing, she reasoned. "I appreciate the thought," she replied stiffly.

"I'll see you at dinner tonight, then. And this time we'll go a little more slowly," he said. Before she could respond, he left.

Standing looking at the door, she frowned. He was a good man, but he obviously wasn't in love with her. He just wasn't certain how to walk away. Considering her weakness for him, it might be best if she never saw him again. "I'll see him tonight. Knowing how he feels should help dampen my ardor. By the end of the evening, I'll probably be entirely cured of him," she told herself in a voice that was more of an order than an observation.

But she didn't see him that evening. At Tanner's request, Frank came to Cactus Anne's that night to apologize and tell her that Tanner's father had suffered a heart attack and he'd had to fly home.

Recalling how fond he was of his father, she'd felt a deep sympathy for the cowboy.

She'd also felt some disappointment. She knew it wasn't realistic, but she hadn't been able to stop herself from hoping that he might learn to care for her.

The next evening a dozen roses arrived from him. "We'll have dinner as soon as I can get back to town," the note said. It was signed simply "Tanner."

But his father's heart attack had been massive. All Tanner's time and attention were required for the running of the ranch and visiting his father in the hospital.

He did call a few times during the next few weeks. He sounded tired and under a great deal of strain. She couldn't help thinking that he was making the calls because he considered them an obligation, not something he really wanted to do. Their conversations were stiff. He asked about her day job and Cactus Anne's. She asked about his father. Their relationship and their future were never discussed.

The feelings of nausea began a couple of weeks after Tanner had left. At first she thought she had a stomach flu. It was one morning at work, a little more than four weeks since he'd been gone, that another possibility entered her mind. At first she tried to deny it, but all day long she kept glancing at her calendar. That evening, she purchased a pregnancy-test kit on her way home. It verified her fears.

She knew that if she told Tanner, he'd insist on marrying her. She was also fairly certain he wasn't in love with her. And he had enough responsibility on his shoulders at the moment. Her streak of independence insisted that she face this on her own. When he called the next time, she told him that someone new had entered her life. He assumed it was another man. When, without argument, he accepted her decision that they shouldn't have anything more to do with one another, she knew she'd done the right thing.

Two weeks later she left Philadelphia and went back to Idaho Falls.

Tanner's image filled Rebecca's groggy mind. Anxiously she wondered how her uncle's meeting with the rancher had gone. Then a sense of overwhelming exhaustion descended over her and she slept.

Awaking slowly a few hours later, Rebecca wondered if her medication had a slightly hallucinogenic effect. She'd been thinking about Tanner earlier, and now the remembered scent of his after-shave seemed to float softly in the air around her.

"It's about time you woke up," Janie greeted her. "You can have a drink as soon as I take your temperature."

The nurse had the thermometer in Rebecca's mouth before her last words were out. Then, following the routine with which Rebecca was becoming familiar, Janie took Rebecca's pulse, fluffed the pillows, straightened the sheets and checked the IV tubes. By the time she'd finished these chores, the thermometer was ready to be read. After recording the results, Janie gave Rebecca the promised drink.

"Can I speak to her now?" an impatient male voice demanded from somewhere behind the nurse.

A tremor ran through Rebecca. She would have recognized that Texas drawl anywhere. She hadn't been hallucinating. Tanner was there.

Janie turned toward the door of the room. "I told you to wait outside, Mr. Lathrop, until I summoned you," she said sternly.

"And I told you that I intended to see her the moment she awoke." Ignoring the dismissal in her tone and expression, Tanner moved farther into the room.

Janie glanced worriedly at Rebecca, then back at Tanner. "Normally only family is allowed to visit patients in intensive care," she said. "Miss Worthen needs her rest."

Tanner's voice became less authoritative and more coaxing. "I've cleared my visit with the doctor. And as I explained to him, Rebecca sent for me."

Janie turned her attention back to Rebecca. "Do you feel strong enough for a visitor at the moment?" she asked gently.

As ordinary visitor, yes. But Tanner was no ordinary visitor. There had been times when she'd wondered what it would be like to see him again. Would the old attraction still be there? She had tried very hard to bury it and convince herself she harbored no lingering feelings for the man. But just knowing he was there was causing her blood to race. Even healthy, she was not certain she was ready to face Tanner again. But she had no choice. "Yes, this is important," she replied.

Janie gave Rebecca a reassuring smile. Then the sternness returned to her expression as she turned toward Tanner. "You may have five minutes, no more."

He nodded his agreement. Removing his Stetson, he approached the bed.

He was dressed nearly the same as he had been the first night she'd seen him—in a well-cut suit, string tie and leather boots. But his face was different. He looked older and wearier, and his expression was harder, giving his features a more chiseled definition. Finding her voice, she said, "Your Texas charm didn't seem to work so well on Janie."

A smile played at one corner of his mouth. "Guess I haven't been as cooperative as I could have been."

Rebecca's breath caught in her throat. It was the same smile Michael used whenever he'd done something he knew he shouldn't have. The phrase "like father, like son" flashed through her mind. She studied Tanner anxiously. His features were shuttered, giving her no clue as to what he was thinking. "How's your father?" she asked.

Grief shadowed his eyes. "He died more than a year ago."

"I'm sorry." She closed her eyes as the desire to sleep again suddenly came over her. Then she forced herself to stay awake. There was something she had to know. "Have you seen Michael?"

There was a pause. Then he said, "No, I came here first."

A guardedness had entered his voice and she wondered what was wrong. It suddenly occurred to her that he didn't want the boy and had come only out of a sense of duty. She knew from experience that was a well-developed trait in his personality. But Michael was too precious to her to allow him to go to anyone who would consider him merely an obligation. Her jaw tensed. "If there's any question in your mind about wanting him, then leave and go back to your ranch. He has Susan and Jack. They love him dearly. I don't want him in an environment where he won't be wanted or loved. He's too special—"

"Get out of here!" Jack snarled as he burst into the room and raced toward the bed. Grabbing Tanner by the arm, he tugged at the rancher, clearly determined to make him leave. "I won't allow the likes of you to come in here and upset my niece."

But Tanner refused to budge. Instead he stood his ground, meeting the older man's anger with an air of challenge. "Seems there was something you forgot to tell me."

Rebecca stared at the two men in confusion. "I

don't understand. Uncle Jack, didn't you tell him about—"

"I didn't tell him anything," Jack cut in sharply, his gaze locked on the Texan.

"Oh," Rebecca groaned weakly. Panic flowed through her.

Janie had followed in Jack's wake. "Both of you get out of here," she ordered. "You're upsetting my patient and I won't stand for it."

Tanner glanced toward Rebecca and frowned with concern. Then his gaze swung back to Jack. "We can finish this discussion in the hall," he conceded. Shaking off Jack's hand, he started toward the door.

"It's already finished," Jack snapped. "Go back to Texas and leave my niece alone."

Tanner paused, his gaze narrowing with purpose as he leveled it on Jack. "I'm not leaving until I know the truth."

"Both of you are leaving this room immediately!" Janie interjected before the men could begin arguing again. Taking each by an arm, she began steering them toward the door.

Rebecca had been watching mutely. She'd made a blunder. A big one. Somehow she had to correct it. "Wait!" she called.

Janie glanced over her shoulder. "You need your

rest," she said soothingly. "I'll make sure these two behave themselves."

Rebecca was frantic with worry about her son. She had to know why Jack hadn't told Tanner. "Please..." she requested, attempting to rise.

Abruptly releasing the two men, Janie rushed back to the bed. "You mustn't try to get up," she admonished, quickly checking the monitors and taking Rebecca's pulse. "You could cause more damage."

"Is she all right?" Tanner demanded harshly, retracing his steps to the bedside.

"As if you really cared," Jack growled, returning to the bed also.

"I want to speak to Tanner alone," Rebecca demanded, the pain from her first attempt to rise keeping her from making a second.

"You're too weak," Janie objected. "And you mustn't allow yourself to get upset."

"It's important," Rebecca insisted.

"He's not worth your time," Jack argued venomously.

Tanner was watching her worriedly. "We can talk later," he said gruffly, beginning to move toward the door.

But Rebecca was too afraid to wait until later. She had to get this straightened out now. "No."

She looked up pleadingly at Janie. "I've got to speak to him now—alone." She met the nurse's gaze levelly. "I may not have another opportunity."

For a long moment the nurse was silent. Then with a comforting smile, she said gently, "All right." But the smile vanished when she turned toward Tanner. "Don't you dare do or say anything to upset my patient any further."

"I won't," he promised.

"You're not staying in here without me," Jack stated, planting his feet firmly.

"Uncle, please," Rebecca said. Her head was beginning to pound and the weariness was threatening to overpower her.

"I think it would be best to let her have her way," Janie said in a coaxing but firm voice.

For a moment Jack hesitated, then nodded. But before leaving, he turned to Tanner and said, "If you bring any harm to my niece, they'll be needing a bed for you in this hospital."

"I didn't come here to cause Rebecca any harm," Tanner replied.

Jack gave a loud, "Hmph," and exited the room.

"I'll be monitoring from the other side of the window," Janie said, her voice carrying a warning as she, too, left the room.

Tanner regarded Rebecca with concern. "Maybe we should talk later," he suggested.

"No." She fought back the urge to drift into the blackness. "I'm confused. Why did you come?"

"To find out what is going on and how I'm involved," he replied.

She tried to remember what she'd said about Michael. Maybe she hadn't revealed too much. Maybe she could bluff her way out of this. "There's been a mistake. You're not involved in any way."

Tanner studied her narrowly. "Who is Michael, Rebecca?"

She tensed. Her uncle must have had a good reason not to tell Tanner about Michael. "He's no one for you to concern yourself with. I didn't mean to disrupt your life. Please, go home and forget about all of this. There is nothing for you here."

"Disrupt my life." His expression darkened and his gaze burned into her as if he was trying to see into her very soul. "Forget about this? Woman, I don't know what is going on in your mind, but I'm not leaving until I know why your uncle came to see me."

The throbbing in her head was making thinking close to impossible, but she was determined to convince Tanner to go back to Texas. "The first time I regained consciousness I was slightly delirious and mentioned your name,'' she lied. ''I told my uncle that I would like to see you if you weren't already married or engaged and if my seeing you wouldn't interfere with your present life. It was foolish of me and I apologize.'' Her body demanded sleep. ''Go home. Go back to your wife or your sweetheart or whoever you left behind,'' she urged. Her eyes closed. ''I feel so tired,'' she murmured, as the darkness began to close in around her.

''I left no one behind.'' Reaching down, Tanner took her hand in his. ''Rebecca.'' He said her name with command. His hold on her hand tightened as if he could will his own strength into her. ''Your uncle took one look at me and determined that he didn't like what he saw. You had something important you wanted him to tell me. What was it?''

Rebecca opened her eyes, but they refused to focus properly. ''I'm too tired to think,'' she murmured. Tanner could be telling the truth. But she had to be careful. Michael's future was in her hands.

''Rebecca, who is Michael?'' Tanner demanded again.

''Michael.'' She smiled dreamily as an image of the dark-haired, blue-eyed child danced in her mind.

''Who is Michael?'' Tanner repeated.

Rebecca's jaw hardened. A surge of strength flowed through her. Opening her eyes, she glared up at him with the protectiveness of a she-wolf fighting for her young. "He's *my* son. Now, please go home, Tanner, and leave us alone." As quickly as the surge of energy had come, it vanished. Her eyes closed and the blackness enveloped her completely.

For a long moment Tanner stood grimly staring down at the woman lying in the bed. Then an expression of cold purpose came over his face and he abruptly left the room.

Hours later, as Rebecca began to awaken again, she wondered if Tanner had actually been there. There was a sort of haze hanging over her mind and sometimes she wasn't certain what was real and what wasn't. His being there could have been a dream, a very vivid one. More like one of those nightmares you wake up from and are relieved to realize *are* nightmares, she corrected. Hoping that his visit had been merely one of those, she opened her eyes.

But if it had been a dream, then she was still dreaming, she thought, seeing him sitting in the lounge chair near the bed. She watched him rise to his feet and look down at her.

"You lied to me, Rebecca," he said in a tightly controlled voice. "I've seen Michael. He's *our* son."

This was no dream. "I didn't lie," she murmured at last. "I simply didn't tell you everything."

"You should have, Rebecca," he growled. "In fact, you should have come to me when you first discovered you were pregnant. I would have married you."

"I know." She faced him with pride. "But I didn't want you to feel trapped into a marriage you would regret."

His expression grew grimmer. "Did you think I was the kind of man who would willingly leave a trail of unwanted bastards?"

"No, or I wouldn't have considered contacting you now," she replied. "But I did know that you didn't love me."

His jaw twitched, giving evidence that he was having a difficult time controlling his temper. "You were pregnant with my child. I had a right to know." His shoulders stiffened. "But what's past is past. I intend to correct this situation immediately. You and I are going to get married, and I'm going to claim Michael legally as my son."

Rebecca forced the shadow of lingering fogginess from her mind as she focused every ounce of her attention sharply on the tall Texan. Before she agreed to this, she needed to be certain of how he felt about Michael. "You said you saw Michael. What did you think of him?"

The anger in his eyes faded, and a loving pride etched itself into his features. "He was dubious of me at first, but he didn't run and hide. He faced me. He's got courage and spunk." Tanner's jaw hardened. "I feel cheated, Rebecca. You kept him from me for two precious years. But from this moment on, I'm going to be a part of his life."

"I did what I thought was right," she said in her defense.

He drew a terse breath. "Now it's time for you to do what *is* right."

She'd always known that Tanner was a good man. The look on his face when he spoke of Michael assured her that he cared deeply for his son. But more importantly, he could assure Michael a good future. "All right," she agreed.

"Tonight," Tanner stipulated.

There was an urgency in his voice, and she knew he was worried she might die before he could make his relationship with Michael legal. But there was one stipulation that had to be made. "I want your word that you'll allow Jack and Susan free access to Michael," she demanded.

"I would not keep him away from people he loves," Tanner assured her.

"I want your word," she repeated.

"You have my word," he replied. "Now rest and I will see you tonight."

"Tonight…" she echoed, then once again drifted into a state of unconsciousness.

The next time she awoke it was to find Tanner at her bedside again. Susan and Jack were there, also, along with the minister from her church. Vaguely she realized the doctor and Janie were also there in the background.

"Came to see him do the right thing by you," Jack said, casting a glare toward Tanner, then smiling softly at Rebecca.

Rebecca felt more exhausted than ever. It was a strain to keep her mind focused on what was happening. "Could we do this quickly?" she requested. "I'm so tired.…"

Susan took Rebecca's hand in hers. "I like your Tanner," she said encouragingly.

He does have a way with women, Rebecca thought, but she couldn't find the strength to make this observation aloud.

Tanner motioned for the minister to begin. The ceremony lasted only a few minutes, but for Rebecca every moment was a struggle to remain conscious. For Michael's sake, however, she managed until she had signed the license and a few other documents Tanner had brought along. A sense of peace came over her as he took the pen from her hand. She'd done what was necessary to ensure that Michael would be taken care of. Breathing a sigh of relief, she closed her eyes and allowed the darkness to gather around her.

"Let her sleep," the doctor said, urging everyone except Janie out of the room.

"I'll stay," Tanner replied, stepping back from the bed to allow Janie room to go through her monitoring routine.

"I'll stay, too," Jack said, his manner making it clear that, although Tanner had done the right thing by his niece, he still didn't trust the man.

"Only one can stay, and legally that should be the husband," the doctor replied, glancing toward Susan for help.

"Come on, dear, we need to get home to Michael," she urged Jack.

"I intend to see that you treat my niece properly," the older man warned Tanner.

"I never meant to treat her improperly in the first place," Tanner replied.

Jack gave a disbelieving snort as he allowed himself to be ushered out.

But Tanner took no notice. He was watching the doctor and the nurse. The moment the doctor had begun ushering everyone out of the room, Janie had gone to the bed and begun her usual patient-monitoring routine. She'd given the doctor a glance that had caused him to return to Rebecca's bedside. Now the nurse and the doctor were conversing quietly.

Tanner waited until the door had closed behind Susan and Jack, then approached the bed. "Is something wrong?" he asked.

The doctor gave him an encouraging smile as he finished jotting down something on Rebecca's chart, which he then handed to the nurse. "Miss Worthen..." He paused and corrected himself. "Mrs. Lathrop has been through a great deal. I'm sure she just needs some rest." Turning back to Janie, he said, "Give me a call if there are any changes."

Tanner watched the man leave, then focused his attention on the nurse. "Now, I want you to tell me the truth," he said curtly.

"The truth is very difficult to know in trauma cases," Janie hedged, avoiding his eyes as she rehung the chart on the foot of the bed. "I'm sure the doctor is right. Mrs. Lathrop had been through a great deal. She just needs rest.''

''I know when someone is lying to me,'' Tanner said warningly. ''You're worried and I want to know why.''

''I worry about all my patients,'' she replied, starting toward the door.

Tanner caught her by the arm, halting her escape. His gaze narrowed on her. ''I want to know what it is specifically about my wife that's worrying you.'' His words were clipped and precise.

Janie glanced back toward the bed and the anxiousness returned to her face. ''Her pulse is a little threadier than it was earlier and her breathing is a little more shallow. I've seen trauma patients give up. Maybe she was just holding on until she was certain of her son's future.''

Tanner released the nurse's arm as the meaning behind her words sunk in. Striding over to the bed, he glared down at the pale brunette lying there. ''You're not going to die on me, Rebecca,'' he growled. ''We've got unfinished business between us.''

Rebecca surfaced groggily. ''We just finished it,'' she said, her speech blurred.

His hand closed around hers as if he could will his strength into her. ''No, we didn't.'' His gaze bored into her. "And there's Michael to consider. He needs you. Can you turn away from him that easily?"

"Go away, Tanner," she requested, her eyelids feeling so heavy she didn't have the energy to keep them open. "I'm tired. So very tired."

"Maybe you've never really loved him," he challenged. "You had him because you felt you had no choice, and you had him alone so you could play the martyr."

Anger gave her strength. Opening her eyes, she glared up at him. "That's not true. I do love him, and I had him because I wanted him!"

Tanner released a harsh breath. "Prove it. Live for him."

"I will," she murmured. "I will."

Chapter Five

And she was going to live. Rebecca knew that now. They had moved her out of intensive care earlier that morning. Now she lay staring up at the ceiling of her private room while her private nurse sat knitting quietly in a chair nearby. The nurse's name was Martha Stuart. Rebecca guessed she was in her early fifties. She was medium in build, grayhaired, her uniform looked starched and her bearing reminded Rebecca of a drill sergeant. She was purported to be an excellent nurse. Tanner had insisted on hiring her. He was determined that Rebecca should have the best possible treatment.

Tanner. She closed her eyes and his image filled

her mind. She'd married him. He knew about Michael and he already had his lawyer making certain that every document, including Michael's birth certificate, had been amended to show that he, Tanner Lathrop, was Michael's father. What next? she wondered worriedly.

As if in answer to her question, the door opened and Tanner entered carrying a large bouquet of red roses. "Thought these might brighten up the room." He glanced toward Martha as he set the vase on the bedside table. "I'd like to speak to my wife privately," he requested politely but firmly.

The nurse set aside her knitting and, rising, looked down at her patient. "Are you feeling up to visitors?"

Not this one, Rebecca answered mentally. But she knew it couldn't be avoided. Aloud she said, "Yes."

"She's still very weak," Martha cautioned Tanner. "I'll go get a cup of coffee, but I won't be gone long."

"I have a favor to ask," Tanner began bluntly as soon as he and Rebecca were alone.

His shoulders were squared as if he expected an argument. Rebecca guessed she wasn't going to like what he was about to ask.

"I have to go back to my ranch for a few days,"

he said evenly. "I want to take Michael with me. We're getting close, and I don't want to disrupt that by suddenly being away from him."

Rebecca's stomach knotted. The idea of his taking Michael to Texas and not bringing him back filled her with terror.

Tanner held up a hand in a sign of peace. "I know that's asking a lot. But I figured I'd ask Susan to come along. Jack can come, too, if he wants. That way Michael won't feel he's being thrust into the midst of strangers."

Rebecca was too weak to be subtle. She told herself that if he was willing to take Susan and Jack along, then he couldn't be planning to steal her son. Still, she needed to hear him say it. "I want your word that you'll bring Michael back."

He scowled. "*I* would never deprive Michael of one of his parents."

Rebecca's jaw tensed at this sharply delivered jab. She'd only done what she thought was right but she was too weak to debate that point at the present time. "All right, you can take him," she conceded.

Tanner drew a relieved breath. "Thanks."

"What's he talked you into now?" an angry male voice demanded from the doorway.

"Jack," Susan admonished, "there's no reason to start a fight."

"He's up to something. I can tell," Jack replied, studying Tanner warily as he approached the bed.

Tanner met the older man's anger with calm control. "I've been arranging with Rebecca for me to take Michael back to Texas with me for a few days."

"No!" Jack stamped his foot for emphasis. He turned toward Rebecca. Concern was etched deeply into his features. "You can't be seriously considering allowing that? What guarantee do you have that he'll bring the boy back?"

The knot in Rebecca's stomach tightened as she saw her own fear reflected in her uncle's eyes. "I have his word," she replied, attempting to keep her tone neutral. "And he's invited you and Aunt Susan to go along."

"I've been there and I've no desire to go back," Jack snarled. "And neither you nor Michael has to go, either." He took Rebecca's hand in his. "You've always got a home with me and Susan. And I've talked to Sam. Your job will be waiting for you whenever you're ready to go back to it."

"Rebecca's my wife and I'll see that she's properly taken care of," Tanner interjected tersely.

Jack glared at him. "And I want her to know she

has options. She didn't need you before and she doesn't have to put up with you now.''

"I'd never take advantage of her or make her do anything she didn't want to do,'' Tanner returned curtly.

Jack raised a cynical eyebrow. "That's open for debate.''

Rebecca flushed. The implication that Michael had been conceived because Tanner had forced himself upon her was strong in Jack's voice. Her fair side insisted that she come to the rancher's defense. "Uncle—''

"Don't go repeating that 'two consenting adults' business,'' Jack snapped, cutting her short. He turned toward Tanner. "She didn't want to marry you then and I don't want her to feel she has to hold to vows she made when she thought she was dying.''

Tanner's gaze swung to Rebecca. "I have no intention of holding her to any vows she doesn't want to be held to.''

The coldness in his eyes made it clear to her that, as far as he was concerned, they had no future together. But then she'd always known that. A sensation that felt like disappointment swept through her. *You can't honestly care,* she admonished herself. Granted, the old attraction was still there. She hated admitting that, but it was the truth. When he walked into a room, his presence was the one that held her attention. But that was only a physical reaction, she assured herself. And, it was what had gotten her into trouble in the first place. Although she loved Michael and would never regret having given birth to him, she wasn't going to allow any weakness for Tanner to complicate her life further or cause her even a moment's grief.

"Jack, I really don't think this is the time or place," Susan cut in, her gaze flicking anxiously over the other occupants in the room. "Sometimes in the heat of anger things get said that shouldn't be said," she added.

Rebecca glanced toward her aunt. There was a curious, underlying edge in Susan's voice. Did her aunt actually believe there was a chance that Rebecca and Tanner could have a real marriage?

"There's nothing but the truth being spoken here," Jack stated.

"Nothing but the truth," Tanner confirmed.

Shades of the truth, Rebecca corrected mentally. It wasn't that she hadn't wanted to marry Tanner. But she had been certain he didn't want to marry her. And the hardness in his features assured her that he had no intention of remaining married to her now. Susan might as well forget any romantic notions she harbored.

"What's going on in here?" Martha demanded, striding into the room. Her gaze swung around the assembly, noting the anger on Jack's and Tanner's faces and the concern on Susan's. She scowled at Tanner. "I warned you that your wife needs her rest. She's still very weak."

And embarrassed and humiliated to boot, Rebecca added silently.

"All of you, out!" Martha ordered, pointing toward the door.

As much as Rebecca would have liked to have been left alone at that moment, the heated exchange coupled with the ice in Tanner's eyes had rekindled her fears. She had to know if she was making the right decision to allow him to take Michael to Texas. "I'd like to speak to my aunt and uncle," she requested before they could be ushered out.

Martha's expression softened as she turned toward Rebecca. "You should rest. You can talk to them later."

"I need to talk to them now," Rebecca insisted.

Martha shook her head but gave a resigned sigh. "All right. But only for a few minutes," she stipulated.

Tanner's eyes filled with distrust. "I'll stay,

too," he said, starting to follow Susan and Jack back to the bed.

"You can wait outside," Martha ordered.

Tanner glared at her. "I'm paying your salary. You'll do as I say."

"You're paying me to take care of your wife to the best of my ability," Martha replied, facing him squarely. "Either you do as *I* say or you can have my resignation."

For a moment he looked as if he might challenge her. But instead, he cast an angry glance toward Jack and left.

Rebecca looked at the nurse. "I have to speak to them alone," she said firmly.

Martha scowled disapprovingly. "If you two care about her health, you'll keep this short and pleasant," she cautioned.

Rebecca waited until the nurse was gone, then she faced her aunt. "I need to know if you have any good reasons for my not allowing Tanner to take Michael to Texas."

"He could take him there and keep him there," Jack said before his wife could speak.

Susan frowned at her husband. "I don't think he'll do that. He cares for the boy and he knows how much Michael loves Rebecca. Even more importantly, he's *promised* me he won't try to take Michael away from her, and I believe him.''

Rebecca trusted Susan's judgment. She admitted to herself that she didn't honestly want to let Tanner take Michael to Texas, but her sense of fair play demanded that she must. She took her aunt's hand in hers. ''Will you go with Michael and Tanner?''

''Of course I will,'' Susan replied. She smiled warmly. ''I've always wanted to see a real ranch.''

Jack's jaw set in a determined line. ''I'll be going, too.''

Tanner *had* invited him, Rebecca reminded herself. It also occurred to her that she would feel safer if Jack was there. But again her sense of fair play came to the fore. Tanner deserved a chance to be a father to his son without having to fight Jack every step of the way. Gently, she took her uncle's hand in hers. ''I need you to stay here with me.''

Jack opened his mouth to argue, but before he could speak, Tanner strode into the room. Approaching the bed, he stood at the foot, his gaze raking over the assemblage. ''If the three of you are plotting to keep my son from me, I'll warn you now, you'll lose.''

The protectiveness in his voice when he said ''my son'' left Rebecca with no doubt that Tanner's commitment to the boy was total. The glimmer of a wish that he could feel that way toward her surfaced, but she stopped it before it could grow into anything solid. She and Tanner had no future together. "We weren't," she replied evenly. "Susan will be going with you to Texas. Jack will be staying here."

Surprise registered on his face. For a moment he looked as if he was having a hard time believing her. Then his eyes softened with gratitude. "Thanks," he said gruffly.

Rebecca felt her heart lurch. *You've got to stop having these reactions to him*, she warned herself.

"I just hope you're doing the right thing," Jack muttered under his breath.

I hope so, too, Rebecca replied silently.

The next day was a nervous one for Rebecca. When the phone rang and she heard Tanner's voice on the other end of the line informing her that they had arrived safely at his ranch, she came close to demanding that he bring Michael back immediately. But she stopped herself.

That evening Susan called. "Tanner had a pony waiting for Michael," her aunt informed her in a voice filled with delight. "And a child-size saddle. Michael loved it. I swear that boy was born to ride.

He nearly walked Tanner's legs off making Tanner take him around and around the corral.''

Fear swept through Rebecca. ''Tanner's being careful not to let Michael get hurt, isn't he? He's not trying to make a cowboy out of him in a day, is he?'' she demanded. ''Michael's only two...''

''Tanner's being very careful,'' Susan assured her. ''He has to be, or the two sisters will come down on him like avenging angels.''

''Two sisters?'' Rebecca frowned in confusion. She had been certain Tanner was an only child.

''There's Helen Eberly, Tanner's housekeeper. And he's hired her sister, Mabel O'Malley, as a sort of nanny for Michael,'' Susan elaborated.

''I vaguely recall his mentioning a house-keeper,'' Rebecca said, her mind drifting back to that dinner years ago. A rush of heat spread through her as she recalled the excitement just the touch of his hand had caused. Angrily, she jerked her mind back to the present. ''Tell me about her,'' she requested.

''Helen's the oldest of the two,'' Susan complied. ''She's fifty-seven, tall, lean as a bean pole and a bit intimidating. I've noticed that the two women who come in daily to do the cleaning and any other chores she has for them are careful not to cross her. She's been here since before Tanner was born,'' she hurried on without a pause, clearly operating on the assumption that the more Rebecca knew about the people at the ranch, the more comfortable she would be about Michael's being there. ''Her husband was a wrangler, whatever that is. Actually, I think it's just a basic cowboy here at the ranch. Anyway, they met when she came to work as a cook. And she still rules over the kitchen. When Tanner's mother died—that was nearly twenty years ago—she became the housekeeper. Her husband died fifteen years ago, but she chose to stay on. She doesn't have any children of her own and I get the feeling she thinks of Tanner as a son.''

''It would seem that Tanner has a fairly extensive household,'' Rebecca observed when her aunt finally paused for a breath.

''It's a big house,'' Susan replied, sounding slightly awed.

Rebecca thought of the two-bedroom apartment she shared with Michael. Her chin tightened. It wasn't very large, but it was cozy and full of love. ''Tell me about the sister he's hired as a nanny,'' she requested.

''Mabel's a widow, too,'' Susan continued. ''She's in her mid-fifties. Lost her husband just a couple of years ago. She has three children and five grandchildren. In a lot of ways she's about as different from Helen as night from day. They certainly don't look alike. Mabel's short, plump and laughs a lot. And there's nothing intimidating about her. I think she's a good choice as nanny.'' She paused a moment, then added, ''Tanner certainly seems determined that Michael will be well looked after.''

Rebecca hung up the phone a little later, after having spoken to Michael. She'd listened to him excitedly telling her all about his new pony, and she had to admit that Tanner could give their son everything. But he couldn't love him any more than she did. The problem was, how were they going to share Michael? Maybe once the shock and newness of having a son wore off, Tanner would get bored with him and agree to a short visit during the summer. After all, Tanner had gotten bored with her quickly enough. This thought brought a scowl of self-reproach. Knowing how he felt toward her, how could she still have lingering stirrings of attraction for him. *I'm just in a weakened state,* she told herself.

And a nervous one, she added as the next couple of days passed with unbearable slowness. The recurring nightmare of her accident came back to haunt her, keeping her from getting her much-needed rest.

By the third day, she was exhausted and taut as a bowstring. But she was feeling stronger. It was now nearly five weeks since the accident. Her cracked ribs and her internal injuries were healing nicely. The doctor said her head injury seemed to be definitely on the mend. As proof, her headache was gone. There was some residual dizziness once in a while, but even that was fading. What she had to work on now was getting her strength back. The doctor and Martha had been encouraging her to walk. She climbed out of bed and paced the floor.

"We could go down to the cafeteria and get you a milk shake," Martha suggested, putting aside her knitting and giving Rebecca her full attention. "You could stand to put on a little weight."

Rebecca paused to glance at herself in the mirror. She looked drawn and pale. The doctor had done a good job with her facial cuts, but she could still easily see the small scars where he'd had to stitch her. He told her that eventually those would fade until they weren't noticeable. But at the moment, they remained, thin, slightly pink-tinted lines. Then there was her hair. It had been shaved off on one side for the operation. Now half her head had hair that hung in a braid midway down her back. The other half was covered by growth that was barely an inch long. "Very trendy," she muttered. No wonder Tanner hadn't kissed her after the minister had pronounced them husband and wife. With all the bandages, two small sets of facial stitches on one cheekbone, IVs running into her and residual bruising around her eyes, she must have been a scary sight. *Even if I'd been in perfect condition, he still wouldn't have been interested in kissing me,* she reminded herself. Her shoulders straightened. *And I'm not interested in being kissed by him!*

Forcing the tall rancher out of her mind, she concentrated on her immediate situation. A milk shake sounded good. Getting out of this room sounded even better. She was just about to agree to Martha's suggestion when the door burst open.

"Susan was worried about you," Tanner said. Michael was in one arm, and Susan was right behind.

The sight of her son brought tears of joy to Rebecca's eyes. "Michael!" she breathed.

"We thought seeing him might cheer you up." Tanner had stopped just inside the door. His gaze raked her. "Should you be out of bed?" he demanded, glancing accusingly toward Martha.

"I only look like I've been in a brawl," Rebecca replied.

"The doctor wants her up and walking," Martha said in her most professional voice.

"I suppose he knows what he's doing," Tanner muttered, sounding unconvinced.

Rebecca's hands went to the belt of her robe to make certain it was secure. He made her feel ugly, and her shoulders stiffened with pride. What Tanner thought of her didn't matter, she told herself, returning her attention to her son. Dressed like Tanner in jeans, a plaid shirt and cowboy boots, with a small gray Stetson hat on his head, the same color as Tanner's, Michael looked like a miniature of his father. He was also watching her with the same dubious expression that the rancher wore.

Tanner stood the boy on the floor, but Michael didn't move toward her. Instead, he remained where he was, clinging to Tanner's leg as if feeling a need for the security holding on to the rancher could provide.

Rebecca's chin threatened to tremble. Even though she'd talked to Michael daily on the phone, she'd known it would take him a moment or two to get used to her again. Still, it hurt. Approaching him, she knelt in front of him to bring herself down to his level. "I've missed you," she said lovingly, reaching out and touching his cheek.

A hint of a smile played at the corners of the boy's mouth.

Rebecca smiled back. "Guess I look a little

scary," she continued. A coaxing plea entered her voice. "I could use a hug."

Momentarily, Michael's hold on Tanner's leg tightened, and he glanced up at his father as if asking for approval. Tanner gave a small nod, and Michael released the leg and went into Rebecca's arms.

The moment of hesitation hurt. But what really worried her was wondering if Michael already felt that he was being forced to choose between his parents. She didn't want him torn that way. But she'd face that problem later. Right now, she wanted only to concentrate on her small son, to hold him, to be close to him.

Sitting on the floor, she drew him into her lap. "Tell me again about your pony," she encouraged, choosing a subject she knew he would enjoy.

Michael began to grin and his eyes sparkled with excitement. In a flurry of jabbering, he complied with her request.

During the next half hour, Michael told her about flying in an airplane, showed her his boots and hat and explored the room. Rebecca remained sitting on the floor so that he could easily come back to her. Besides, she didn't have the strength to chase him around the room. *But I will very soon,* she vowed.

"The doctor said fifteen minutes," Susan said, her voice filled with regret. "We've already gone well past that."

Rebecca had to admit she was tired, but she wasn't ready for Michael to leave. "Not yet," she pleaded.

Susan knelt in front of her. Gently she touched her niece's face. "I don't want you overexerting yourself and having a relapse."

"Susan's right," Tanner interjected before Rebecca could lodge a further protest. "Time to go, son," he said.

Michael looked as if he were going to argue.

"How about if you, Aunt Susan and Martha go have an ice-cream cone," Tanner suggested.

Michael grinned. Ice cream was always a sure bribe with him, Rebecca recalled. She'd used it a hundred times herself.

Tanner's gaze shifted to the women. "I'll stay with Rebecca." His voice was polite, but there was no question he was ordering them out of the room.

Both Susan and Martha glanced toward Rebecca worriedly. She was still seated on the floor.

"Rebecca looks tired," Susan said, her tone suggesting that maybe he should allow her niece to rest.

Martha started toward her patient. "I'll just stay and get her tucked back into bed."

Tanner scowled at them impatiently. "I want a few words in private with my wife. I promised I won't tire her." Before Martha could reach Rebecca, he bent, put his hands around Rebecca's waist and lifted her to her feet. "And I can get her back into bed myself."

Rebecca's breath momentarily locked in her lungs as Tanner's touch sent a searing surge of heat through her. Even though she'd been forced to admit to feeling a lingering attraction for him, she'd been sure he could never rekindle the fire he'd once started. But she'd been wrong. Her pride, however, refused to allow him to know that. "I can get myself back into bed just fine," she said, steeling herself to move away from his touch with slow dignity rather than jerking away. She also didn't want him or the other two women thinking that she felt any need to be protected from him. With a mask of cool indifference in place, she turned toward her aunt and then to Martha. "I would appreciate if you two would take Michael for ice cream."

"Ice cream," the child repeated with a grin.

"All right," Susan conceded, still looking doubtful.

"Don't tire her," Martha warned Tanner sternly.

Rebecca gave Michael a final hug, then started toward the bed. Halfway there she stopped. The sudden thought of facing Tanner from her bed had a disconcerting effect on her. Changing direction, she went to the chair Martha had been using and seated herself. She supposed that Tanner was going to ask her if he could take Michael back to his ranch for another visit in the near future.

Tanner remained standing several feel from her. He waited until they were alone, then he said, "It hurt, didn't it?"

Rebecca frowned in confusion. Her body was still sore and moving around caused some pain, but she had the feeling that wasn't what he was talking about.

"Not having Michael run into your arms," he elaborated. "Having to get reacquainted with him as if you were, for a moment, a stranger."

She glared at him. "Of course it hurt. But it was understandable. He hasn't seen me for weeks, and I know I look different, probably even a little frightening with this weird hairdo." Self-consciously, her hand went up to the side of her head where the hair was short.

The hint of a smile played at the corners of Tanner's mouth. "It is a rather interesting effect. Sort of futuristic, maybe punk. But not unattractive."

Rebecca stared at him. He'd paid her a compliment. Even more, there was a sudden warmth in his eyes that caused her pulse to quicken.

Then he frowned and his expression turned cold. *His attraction to me has never been any more than surface,* she reminded herself. It was easy for him to brush it aside. *And these flashes of attraction I keep having toward him are only surface, too,* she affirmed.

"However, I didn't come here to talk about your hair," he went on. His gaze leveled on her. "I don't want Michael to have to readjust to me every few weeks. I want a chance to be a full-time father. I've given this a lot of thought. Unless you're keeping secrets from your aunt, you have no romantic involvements that would interfere with continuing our marriage. Therefore, it is my intention that we should attempt to make this marriage work."

Shock registered on her face. "Stay married?" she choked out. She'd been certain he was already having his lawyers draw up divorce papers.

"I would not expect to exercise all my husbandly prerogatives immediately," he continued in a businesslike manner. "I figured we'd take time to get to know one another and see if we think this can work."

Rebecca felt the same chill she'd felt when he'd

proposed marriage to her that morning three years ago. He didn't really want to be married to her. What he wanted was his son. ''Marriages for the sake of children generally don't last, nor are they healthy,'' she said stiffly.

His jaw hardened. ''We can be the exception.'' He moved toward her until he was standing directly in front of her. ''I want the chance, Rebecca. If you won't agree, I'll go to court and fight for joint custody. You'll have him for six months out of the year and I'll have him for six months.''

The thought of not being with her son for six months at a time caused Rebecca's stomach to knot. ''You wouldn't...you can't.''

''I will and I can,'' he assured her. ''I missed the first two years of his life. I will not willingly miss any more.''

Looking up into his hard, determined features, Rebecca felt trapped. She knew this marriage wasn't going to work. But it was equally obvious that arguing with Tanner wasn't going to do any good. ''What if we aren't compatible?'' she asked.

The blue of his eyes deepened to the shade of midnight. Placing a hand on either arm of the chair, he leaned down until only inches separated their faces. ''We were compatible enough in the past.''

The blue depths of his eyes took her back to another place, another time. His remembered kisses taunted her while his breath teased her skin, sending currents of heated excitement racing through her. She couldn't believe that all he had to do was get close and her body flamed with desire. And he knew it! She saw the look of triumph on his face. Self-directed fury raged through her. How could she still be so weak! Hadn't she learned her lesson?

"Like I told you before, for me, sharing a bed isn't all there is to a marriage," she snarled. "I want a husband who'll be my friend, my companion."

He straightened away from her, a coolness descending over his features once again. "I'm willing to give it a try."

How could he be so hardheaded? "And what do you figure our odds of making it work are?" she challenged.

He shrugged. "About one in a million. But I still figure it's worth a try."

Chapter Six

Rebecca paced the living-room floor in Susan and Jack's house. It was now eight weeks since her accident. Once she had begun on the road to recovery, her health had improved rapidly. Her face was still a bit pale but more normal in color. She'd had her hair cut into a short bob. It felt odd not being long, but she consoled herself with the realization that eventually it would grow out. In the meantime, this new look was more in keeping with her traditional, conservative nature.

A little over a week ago she'd been released from the hospital. She'd had no apartment to return to. Tanner had already gotten her out of her lease and, other than the necessary personal items and some clothing, had all of her and Michael's belongings shipped to Texas. However, pointing out that Rebecca was still tiring easily and had not regained her full strength, Susan had requested that Rebecca be allowed to come home with her for a while. Tanner had raised no objections. Thus, since she'd left the hospital, Rebecca had been staying with Susan and Jack, recuperating and getting reacquainted with her son.

But Tanner had not remained with her and Michael in Idaho Falls. Explaining that he had pressing business to attend to, he'd flow back to his ranch.

Rebecca scowled at the clock. It was midafternoon. She continued to pace restlessly. She was tired of this limbo in which she was living. A small, cynical smile played at one corner of her mouth as she wondered if Tanner had changed his mind about their marriage. When he'd been around, he'd behaved politely but detached toward her. "He's probably having my things shipped back up here right now," she muttered. The thought should have brought a sense of relief. Instead it only made her more tense. "That's because I'm worried about how we'll handle Michael," she reasoned.

"The way you're pacing and muttering to yourself, I'd say you have something important on your mind.''

Rebecca jerked around to discover Tanner entering the room. Her pulse immediately quickened. Damn, why did she have to find the man so attractive! There were other men who were more handsome. But none of them could spark her interest the way Tanner did. *You'd think you would've learned your lesson,* she berated herself. "I didn't expect you back until tomorrow.'' She'd meant to sound cool and indifferent. Instead there was a nervous catch in her voice. She scowled to cover it.

"A wife is supposed to at least act pleased to see her husband,'' he admonished dryly.

I would be if my husband wanted to be my husband, she returned mentally. The sudden thought of rushing into Tanner's waiting arms caused a heat to spread through her. She turned away from him as self-directed anger cooled it. *My reactions to him are purely physical,* she again affirmed. She took a deep, calming breath, then turned back. "It's time for me to get on with my life, Tanner.''

His jaw firmed. "I'm glad to hear you say that, because being away from my ranch so often makes it difficult for me to conduct my business the way I want to. We'll leave tomorrow.'' He glanced toward the stairs. "And now that that's settled, if you'll excuse me, I'll go find my son. I assume he's in his room napping?''

''Yes,'' she replied absently to his already departing back.

For the rest of the afternoon, evening, night and into the next morning, she held a running debate with herself. This was her last chance to call a halt to Tanner's plans to attempt to make their marriage work. But when the time came to leave with him, she went.

Sitting in the window seat of the private jet he'd chartered, she feigned an interest in the landscape passing below. Beside her, Michael slept peacefully. She wasn't certain why she was there. She'd told herself a hundred times it was for Michael's sake. She didn't want her son being torn between two parents, having his life disrupted every six months by being moved from one household to the other. But her more practical side told her that was going to happen, anyway. Neither she nor Tanner nor Jack nor Susan honestly expected this marriage to work. ''One chance in a million,'' Tanner had said. Jack, too, had been blatant about his skepticism.

''You don't have to go with him,'' he'd told her when she informed him and Susan the night before that she would be leaving with Tanner in the morning. When she'd held firm to this decision, Jack had added that she and Michael would always have a place in his home whenever they were ready to return.

Susan had been less openly pessimistic. "I hope this works out the way you want it to," she'd said. Then she'd also added that Rebecca and Michael would always have a place in her and Jack's home if they should ever want it.

Rebecca glanced toward Tanner. He was seated across the aisle. His chair was positioned in as much of a reclining posture as possible. His legs were stretched out into the aisle and crossed at the ankle. His hands were folded in his lap. His Stetson was pushed down over his face and, like his son, he was sleeping. As her gaze traveled along the sturdy length of him, she admitted that he was the major reason she was here. She needed to get him out of her system once and for all. Just sitting there looking at him caused her blood to race faster. *But living with him on a day-to-day basis should be a cure,* she reasoned. Continuous exposure would cause her to start finding him boring and his faults annoying.

But at the moment, all she was feeling was nervous. Susan had assured her that she would like the two sisters. But would they like her? Or would they feel they had to choose sides and champion Tanner?

She'd gathered from Susan that both women were very fond of him, although Mabel was somewhat cowed by him.

Tanner suddenly straightened. Pushing his hat back from his face, he scowled impatiently at her. "I wish you'd stop looking at me as if I was a serpent you had to fear," he growled. "I'm only asking for a chance for us to be a family. I gave you my word I wouldn't make any demands on you that you weren't willing to accept."

She'd been certain he was asleep. Her shoulders squared. She refused to allow him to think that he intimidated her. "I'm just a little nervous about how I'll be accepted in your home," she said coolly.

His scowl deepened. "You'll be accepted just fine. You're my wife." His gaze narrowed on her. "And it's *our* home."

She'd greeted this statement with a skeptically raised eyebrow and turned her attention back to the view beyond the window. It was his home and it was Michael's home, but it remained to be seen if she'd be accepted as a welcome member of the household.

"And it still remains to be seen," she muttered to herself. She, Tanner and Michael had arrived at the ranch a short while earlier.

The sisters had greeted her with polite but re-
served smiles. She'd also been introduced to Sally
Jones and Leigh Bluefeather. Both, she guessed,
were in their twenties, and they seemed pleasant.
They were the two women her aunt had mentioned
who came in daily during the week to do the cleaning and odd chores. Both were wives of wranglers
on the ranch and both had been openly curious. But
they'd said little and had remained only a moment
for their introductions before going off to complete
whatever task they'd been working on when Tanner, Rebecca and Michael had arrived.

At least none of them were hostile, she thought,
trying to look on the bright side, as her gaze traveled around the bedroom.

It was her room—her private room. All her
things were here. There were the pictures of her
parents, Michael, Susan, Jack and herself that had
been in the bedroom of her apartment. Her collec-
tion of perfume bottles sat neatly arranged on the
dresser. She opened the closet door to find her
clothes hanging there and her shoes lined up on the
floor. Even the clutter of old memorabilia, hobbies
and general assorted junk that had been stashed on
the shelf in her closet of the apartment in Idaho
Falls now filled the shelf of this closet. Still, there

was no sense of warmth in the room, no feeling of homecoming.

She'd expected to be sharing Tanner's room. But then he'd given her his word that he wouldn't make any immediate demands on her. Or maybe he was having a hard time resurrecting his attraction toward her, she mused. Furious with herself for even caring, she scowled. This marriage wasn't going to work. She was more certain of that by the minute. But she *had* hoped a second exposure to his lovemaking would put an end to the recurring moments of lingering desire she felt for him. She was sure the only reason she remembered their lovemaking as being so exciting was because it was the first time...the only time.

Suddenly she felt as if the walls were closing in on her. Quickly, she changed into a pair of jeans, a shirt and sneakers. Then, leaving the room, she went in search of Michael. She'd left him in the nursery with Mabel. She hadn't wanted to. But he'd rushed over to play with a favorite toy, and Helen had been waiting at the door to show Rebecca to her room. It would have looked foolish of her to insist that Michael accompany them when Mabel was there to watch over him.

Michael, however, wasn't in the nursery. The two sisters were there alone.

"She seems nice," Mabel was saying in motherly tones. "We'll need to take good care of her. We did promise Susan we would. She's still pale and a bit too thin."

Rebecca breathed a silent sigh of relief. At least Mabel was willing to be friendly. But as she gave a sharp knock on the open door to let them know she was there and then entered the room, she caught a glimpse of the skepticism on the older sister's face before it could be masked by an expression of polite deference. Helen, obviously, did not share her sister's benevolent attitude.

"I was looking for Michael," Rebecca said.

"Tanner took him out to the corral for a ride on his pony," Helen informed her. "I'm to give you a quick tour of the house, then take you to join them."

Despite the fact that the housekeeper showed no overt hostility, Rebecca had the sensation of being in enemy territory. Her aunt had been right—the woman did have an intimidating air. The urge to insist that she be taken directly to Michael was strong. The desire to order Tanner to have her and Michael flown immediately back to Idaho Falls was even stronger. Unconsciously, she took a step back.

"Helen, really, you could be a bit less stiff," Mabel admonished. "You can be quite frightening at times without meaning to."

Helen tossed her sister an annoyed glance, then turned back to Rebecca. "I'm a straightforward person," she said crisply. "I liked your aunt and she likes you, so I'm willing to give you a chance."

"Helen! Really!" Mabel exclaimed. "You…"

Helen silenced her sister with a warning glance. "I'm clearing the air," she said firmly, then returned her attention to Rebecca. "I've spent a lifetime saying what I think. Tanner requested that I be a little less blunt with you, but I'm too old to change my ways."

Rebecca met the woman's gaze levelly. "I prefer the bluntness." She was not certain she would like what she heard, but at least she would know exactly where she stood with the housekeeper.

"You'll probably regret having said that," Mabel muttered only to be again silenced by another threatening glance from Helen.

Returning her attention to Rebecca, the housekeeper continued, "I don't know what happened between you and Tanner that would cause you to go off and have his child without telling him. That's between the two of you. But I do know that he's a good man. I'm not claiming he's perfect. He can be right difficult at times. But he's a man a woman should be proud to have as a husband and he's damn good father material.''

"You don't have to curse," Mabel said, frowning at her sister, then glancing toward Rebecca apologetically. But both women ignored her.

Instead, Rebecca continued to meet Helen's gaze. "I have never doubted that Tanner was a good man nor that he would make some woman a good husband."

"Well spoken," a male voice commended dryly from the doorway, followed by a clapping of hands.

Rebecca swung around to find Tanner regarding her as if he didn't believe she meant a word of what she had just said. Then his gaze shifted to Helen. "So much for requesting that you treat Rebecca with kid gloves," he observed disgruntledly.

"I've never been the soft-leather type," Helen replied, her back straightening to let him know that he couldn't intimidate her. "I'm the work-glove type and I don't—"

"And you don't plan to change now," he finished for her, his tone implying that he was familiar with this statement.

"You know what they say about teaching old dogs new tricks," Mabel said, attempting to come to her sister's defense.

Helen swung toward her. "I don't think I like being compared to an old dog."

"If the shoe fits..." Mabel returned.

Tanner stood shaking his head as if he'd heard all this before. "I want you two to take Michael down to the kitchen and feed him some milk and cookies," he ordered, cutting short the sisters' sniping.

Recovering from the shock of Tanner's unexpected appearance, Rebecca saw her son standing a little behind the cowboy. "I'll take him," she said, moving toward the door.

Tanner blocked her way. "You and I need to have a talk."

The determined set of his jaw told her that she had no choice. She could escape from him now, but she'd only have to face whatever he had to say later. Her shoulders stiffened. Might as well get it over with, she decided.

"It's been a long day for Rebecca," Helen's voice cut in before Rebecca could respond. "I think she should rest for a while now. You can talk to her later."

Startled by the woman's unexpected championship, Rebecca glanced at her.

Tanner's gaze, too, shifted to his housekeeper.

"She's my wife and I'll decide when she needs to rest," he growled.

"We promised her aunt we'd look after her," Mabel choked out, fear readable in her eyes.

Clearly she was intimidated by Tanner just as Susan had said, Rebecca observed. Still, she'd attempted to face up to him for Rebecca's sake. The fact that both women had made an attempt to come to her aid gave Rebecca added courage. Maybe this wasn't enemy territory, after all. "I'm fine," she assured them. "Go ahead and take Michael down for some cookies and milk. I'll be along shortly."

"What happened to *your* kid gloves?" Helen asked under her breath as she passed Tanner and offered Michael her hand.

He met the jab with a dry smirk. "Guess you've had a bigger influence on me than I thought."

Michael looked up at Rebecca worriedly as if he wasn't certain what was going on, but wasn't sure he should leave her. "Run along," she said with an encouraging smile.

Mabel reached down and took his hand. "I made your favorite cookies this morning—chocolate chip."

Michael beamed up at her and, taking Helen's hand in his other hand, went with them down the hall.

Tanner closed the door with a nudge from the heel of his boot. Studying Rebecca, he said, "A person could almost believe you meant what you said to Helen. Your skill at lying has improved."

She glared at him defiantly. "I did mean it."

Cynicism etched itself into his features. "In other words, I'd make some woman a good husband as long as it wasn't you."

If he'd loved her... She cut the thought off. He hadn't and he didn't and there was no sense in dwelling on what might have been. She met his gaze evenly. "I've always thought a man should be in love with his wife."

"And vice versa," he added dryly.

"And vice versa," she conceded.

His jaw hardened. "That brings me to a question that's been needling me," he said curtly. "I'd planned to try to forget it—leave the past in the past. But it won't go away. I've decided that Helen's right. It's best to clear the air." Cold anger etched itself into his features. "It has occurred to me that when you discovered you were pregnant with Michael, one of the reasons you didn't tell me was because you thought your new boyfriend would marry you, anyway. Were you planning to let some other man raise my son as his?"

This accusation stung. Her shoulders straightened defiantly. "There was no new boyfriend."

An edge of threat entered his voice. "Don't lie to me, Rebecca. It may be a little vague, but I still recall that last phone conversation we had two and half years ago. You made it clear that you had found a new 'interest.'"

This was the second time in less than ten minutes that he'd called her a liar. Maybe she hadn't been totally fair back then, but she'd done what she'd thought was right. She didn't deserve to be treated as if she had no scruples. She glared at him with self-righteous indignation. "Michael was my new interest. I didn't have any time to think about anything but the impending birth of my child. I was too busy having morning sickness and evening sickness. *And* trying to figure out how I was going to support myself and my baby. *And* wondering how I was going to tell my aunt and uncle. I knew they'd be disappointed in me." Abruptly she stopped herself. She'd never meant to tell him any of this.

"I would have been there for you," he growled, the hint of threat replaced by angry frustration. "You should have told me. I had a right to know. I would have married you and taken care of you."

Pride glistened in her eyes. "But only out of a

sense of duty, not because you really wanted to marry me.''

He drew a terse breath. "The 'whys' are unimportant. I would have married you. You didn't have to face having Michael alone."

Again he'd confirmed what she already knew. He hadn't been in love with her then and he hadn't had any illusions that he might ever be. She'd been merely an evening's entertainment. A wave of indignant anger washed over her. Then she reminded herself that the enjoyment had been two-sided. It would be unfair to blame him for what happened. "Well, I did face it alone," she returned coolly. The determination of a mother fighting for her young spread over her features. "And I love my son. I won't give him up."

Tanner studied her narrowly. "Then I guess we'll just have to make this marriage work, because I won't give him up, either." He motioned toward the door. "I believe *our* son is waiting for us in the kitchen. He wants to introduce you to his pony."

Accompanying Tanner down the stairs, Rebecca glanced over at him. The taut set of his jaw reminded her of a man caught in a trap he wanted out of. *I give this marriage less than two weeks,* she wagered mentally.

But a little later, she had to admit that Tanner

was determined that their union would last. "You'll need to learn to ride, too," he told her when they went down to the stables. Stopping at the fourth stall, he patted the neck of the roan mare inside. "This is Strawberry. She's yours. She's gentle as a lamb. As soon as you feel strong enough we'll begin your lessons."

And after dinner, he took her into his study. "I had these sent out here for you to choose from," he informed her as they entered. On the floor next to the leather couch were several stacks of boxes. Some contained finely tooled cowboy boots, and others housed an assortment of various-colored Stetsons. "I'll have a pair of boots custom-made for you later," he said, motioning for her to be seated. "In the meantime, one or two of these should fit you. Those boots you have left from your job at Cactus Anne's aren't sturdy enough."

Opening the first box, he took out a pair of boots. His manner coolly businesslike, he then removed the tennis shoes she was wearing. As his fingers brushed her ankles, currents of heat shot up her legs. She was barely recovering from this uninvited reaction when he began to slip a boot onto her right foot. Holding on to the loops at the top of the boot, he began to pull it upward. This brought his hands into contact with her calves. The heat she had experienced a moment earlier grew stronger. She glanced at Tanner. There was nothing in his expression or manner to indicate that he found her more interesting than any of the inanimate objects in the room. And he probably found her less interesting than some, she mused, infuriated that he could spark such strong responses in her and yet apparently feel nothing himself. The desire to jerk her leg away from him was close to overwhelming. But pride helped her maintain control. "I can do that myself," she said evenly, easing her leg away from him.

He shrugged as if it made no difference to him and, releasing his hold on the boot, stepped back to give her room.

For the next hour, she tried on boots and hats. Four of the pairs of boots fit nicely, but she refused to keep more than two. He also insisted that she choose two hats in case she should lose one.

"He was generous to a fault." The statement came out sounding like an accusation. She'd tucked Michael in for the night and, leaving him in Mabel's capable hands, had retired to her room. But even alone, away from Tanner, she couldn't relax. She'd ordered herself not to think about the man, but that had been an exercise in futility. Her rational side knew it wasn't fair to be angry with him. He was trying to make the best of a difficult situation. It wasn't his fault if he was no longer attracted to her.

"No doubt he's forgotten I'm even here," she muttered. Her gaze fell on the birth-control pills on the dresser. They were certainly unnecessary. The doctor had suggested that she take precautions against getting pregnant until her body had fully recovered.

A cynical smile tilted the corners of her mouth as she recalled Tanner's reaction to the pills. Without reservation, he'd given his nod of approval. "It would be best not to complicate our lives at the moment with another pregnancy," he'd said, adding a second reason for their use.

She scowled. Tanner had obviously opted for an even safer method—abstinence. Her estimate of how long this marriage was going to last diminished by a week.

Exhaustion seemed suddenly to overwhelm her and she went to bed. But sleep didn't come easily, and when it did, it brought terror with it. She was trapped in her car again. She could smell gasoline fumes and hear Michael calling out to her. She tried to get to him, but she was penned between her seat and the steering wheel. At first she felt numb, then there was excruciating pain. Michael was sobbing now. Afraid the car might burst into flames, she called out to him, telling him to get out.

Another voice entered her nightmare. It held authority. ''Rebecca, wake up,'' it was ordering. ''You're dreaming.''

Tanner's image entered her dream. He was kneeling beside the car. ''Michael's safe,'' he was telling her. ''You're safe,'' he assured her.

He wrapped his arms around her and drew her up against his chest. A warmth spread through her, and a sense of security enveloped her. He stroked her hair, and his hold on her tightened even more. The fear, along with the memories of the pain, subsided.

She circled her arms around him, wanting to hold on to this feeling of warmth and safety forever. Beneath her cheek the crisp hairs of his chest had an intoxicating effect as she snuggled against him.

Her breathing had been coming in gasps. Now it slowed to a more normal rate. He was massaging her back, and it occurred to her that if she were a cat, she would be purring.

Slowly her own palms moved over the sturdy musculature of his back. It felt so real. She turned her face slightly to kiss his chest and the rough hairs tickled her nose.

"Rebecca, wake up," he ordered gruffly.

Her mouth formed a pout. She didn't want to wake up. She wanted to hang on to this illusion. She groaned lightly, fighting the return to reality.

"Rebecca." He sounded impatient and a little angry.

The muscles beneath her palms stiffened, and the embrace in which she had been held slackened. She breathed a regretful sigh. There was no reason to cling to this illusion any longer. But as her mind surfaced, instead of fading into nothingness the sensation of holding on to Tanner grew more real. Beneath her cheek her pillow actually felt like his chest. Frowning in groggy confusion, she slowly opened one eye. The eyelashes combated with crisp curly hairs. A wave of shock washed over her.

This was no illusion! Tanner was there, shirtless and bootless, dressed only in a pair of jeans. Abruptly, she released her hold.

Tanner had been continuing to hold her loosely. Now he unwrapped his arms from around her. "That must have been one hell of a nightmare you were having," he said with an edge of impatience. Grasping her upper arms with his hands, he eased her back onto her pillow.

He couldn't get me out of his embrace fast enough, she thought as he released her.

"I heard you cry out," he added as if his presence in her room required an explanation.

She felt like an idiot. She'd enjoyed being in his arms. But it was obvious he would rather be anywhere else. "It's a recurring nightmare I have about the accident. The doctor says it will go away in time," she replied. Along with the mention of the accident came the sharp image of her son. "Michael," she muttered worriedly and sat up once again. "I'd better check to see if I woke him."

"Go back to sleep," Tanner ordered. He had risen but was continuing to stand beside the bed, blocking her getting up. "Both Michael and Mabel are sleeping soundly," he assured her. "I was still awake. That's why I heard you."

The lingering hint of impatience in his voice caused her to guess that he was sorry he hadn't been asleep, too. It was obvious he wanted to get away from her as quickly as possible. Her shoulders straightened with pride. "If you don't mind, I'll just check on my son, anyway," she said, her tone ordering him to move out of her way.

He gave a shrug as if to say that, in his opinion, checking on Michael was unnecessary, but she could do whatever she wanted. Then he strode out of the room.

Throwing off her covers, Rebecca rose. How

could she have felt so comfortable, so secure, in his arms? He didn't want her there. She was beginning to feel very certain he didn't even want her in his home. Grabbing up her robe, she jerked it on. Her self-directed anger growing by the minute, she didn't bother to belt it as she strode out into the hall. Immediately, she regretted the rashness of this act.

Tanner was standing there at the door of his room watching her. The hall light was on, giving her a clear view of his broad, unclothed chest and shoulders. Against her will a fire sparked inside of her. Furious that she was still suffering from a wanton weakness toward the man, she grabbed the edges of her robe and wrapped the garment tightly around herself. He scowled as if he found this action on her part to be childishly immature.

It wouldn't have mattered if I'd been entirely nude, she chided herself; he had no interest in her. She tossed him a defiant glare and continued toward Michael's room.

Inside the room, she stood beside her son's bed, gazing down at him. He looked so peaceful and so happy. Reaching down, she gently touched his cheek. "I'm sorry," she said softly, "but I really don't think this marriage is going to work."

"Is everything all right?" a woman's voice questioned in low, worried tones.

Rebecca glanced over her shoulder to see Mabel standing in the doorway of the bathroom that connected Michael's room with hers. "Everything's fine," she lied, adding honestly, "I'm sorry I woke you." Then, giving Michael's covers one last little tuck, she said, "Good night," and left.

Tanner was leaning against the doorjamb of his room, still dressed only in his jeans. "Is Michael okay?" he asked as she crossed the hall.

Still intensely irritated with her physical attraction to him, she'd been intending to ignore him. "You were right—he's sleeping peacefully," she replied, continuing toward her room without even a glance in his direction. But as she reached the entrance of her room, a hand closed around her arm, bringing her to a halt. Its callused strength stirred an excitement deep within her while the heat of the contact burned into her. Jerking around, she found herself staring up into the shuttered blue depths of Tanner's eyes.

"Are you all right?" he asked gruffly. "That must be one hell of a nightmare."

"It is," she confirmed. His gaze was softening, and her legs were beginning to feel strangely weak. Maybe he did care for her, at least a little. Then she saw it—sympathy. She knew it wasn't fair to be angry with him for having humanitarian feelings for her, but she couldn't help herself. She didn't want his pity! her body stiffened. Her gaze shifted to the hand still holding her arm, and she frowned at it as if it were an unwanted nuisance. "I'm very tired. Good night," she said with cool dismissal.

Releasing his hold, his manner became distant. "Good night," he replied, and turning away, he strode back across the hall and into his room.

She entered her room and closed the door, wishing she could close him out of her mind as easily. In an attempt to brush off the lingering feel of his touch, she rubbed the spot on her arm where he'd held her. She hated the thought that the only caring emotion he'd exhibited toward her had been sympathy. "One more day should be my limit for enduring him," she stipulated under her breath as she climbed back into bed.

Chapter Seven

Delayed exhaustion from the trip and a restless night caused Rebecca to oversleep the next morning. When she finally awoke it was nearly ten. Her first thought was Michael. But she knew she didn't have to worry. Mabel would be looking after him like a brood hen watching her chick. Her next thought was Tanner. She guessed he would already be out of the house. That, at least, would be a relief. She was in no mood to face him this morning.

Dragging herself out of bed, she dressed in jeans and a lightweight long-sleeved shirt. Here in west Texas the days were hot, but the sun was too strong to go out without adequate covering.

For a long moment she stood staring at the boots Tanner had provided. Her mouth formed a pout. The thought of wearing anything he had bought her irked her, and she opted for a pair of old sneakers, instead. She did, however, take one of the hats as she left the room. She might be irked, but she wasn't stupid.

Stopping at Michael's room, she was not surprised to find it empty. Going down to the kitchen, she found her son and the two sisters around the long table that occupied a central position in the large room. Mabel was seated, drinking coffee, and Helen was kneading bread. Michael was standing on a short stool, trying to imitate the housekeeper's motions with a smaller piece of dough.

As Rebecca entered, he glanced toward her and beamed happily. "Making bread," he informed her with pride.

Both sisters looked up and smiled in polite greeting.

"Sorry I overslept," Rebecca said moving toward the table. She felt embarrassed. Obviously they had all been up for hours. "I'm usually up much earlier," she added.

"Now, don't you fret," Mabel admonished motheringly. "You need your rest." The concern on her face deepened. "You also need a little fattening up. How about some eggs and bacon for breakfast? You sit here and keep an eye on Michael, and I'll have it ready in no time.'' Mabel was already rising from her chair as she spoke.

As an automatic response, Rebecca started to refuse. But the thought of the food caused her mouth to water. She was hungry. She didn't, however, want these women to feel she needed to be waited on. ''Sounds good,'' she said. ''But I can fix it myself.''

''No need for that,'' Helen interjected with authority. ''The both of you sit down. The bread is ready to rise. I'll do the cooking.'' She glanced at her sister. ''You always overdo the eggs and burn the bacon.''

It was obvious Helen considered the kitchen her domain. And it was, Rebecca reminded herself. Not wanting to cause any trouble, she said politely, ''Thank you,'' and turned her attention to Michael.

''Have it your way,'' Mabel replied with a shrug, and started to seat herself once again.

Helen gave her a sharp glance. ''You could offer Mrs. Lathrop a cup of coffee before you make yourself comfortable,'' she suggested in a tone that was more a command than a request.

Mrs. Lathrop. The name caused an unpleasant twist in Rebecca's stomach. Tanner didn't want her for his wife, and she didn't want his name. "Please call me Rebecca," she said.

Mabel tossed her sister an impatient grimace. Then she turned and smiled at Rebecca. "I've always been partial to that name. My oldest daughter is named Katherine Rebecca—"

"Mabel, as much as I adore hearing about my nieces and nephews," Helen interrupted pointedly, "I'm sure Rebecca would like to have a cup of coffee before you begin reciting family history."

Mabel flushed. "I was just trying to make her feel at home," she snapped, glancing over her shoulder at her sister. Turning back to Rebecca, she smiled broadly. "Would you like milk or sugar with your coffee, or both?" Then, as if a thought that would put her a step ahead of her sister had just struck her, she added, "Or would you prefer tea?"

"Coffee with milk will suit me just fine," Rebecca replied. "And I can get it myself."

"No, no. Let me," Mabel insisted, looking mildly disappointed that she hadn't bested her sister. "You just sit down and let Michael show you how well he's learned to knead bread."

Deciding the prudent thing to do would be to obey, Rebecca seated herself near her son.

Michael looked up and grinned at her. Clearly he

was used to the sisters and their exchanges and paid no attention to them. "Bread," he said, holding up the baseball-sized lump he'd been working on.

"Bread," she confirmed, giving him a light kiss on the tip of his nose. Here in this western setting he looked even more like his father. He looked as if he belonged.

"Tanner's out riding fence this morning," Helen said as she fried the bacon. "He'll be back in time for lunch, though. Said if you wanted to go riding with him and Michael, he'd take the two of you out this evening. Afternoon's going to be too hot."

Having made this announcement, Helen concentrated on her cooking while Rebecca sipped her coffee and played with Michael.

But as Helen placed Rebecca's breakfast in front of her, Rebecca noticed a change in the housekeeper's manner. It became more staid. "I should have asked if you wanted to be served in here or in the dining room," she said in a sort of deferential apology.

"In here is fine," Rebecca assured her, the fact that she was, at the moment, mistress of this house suddenly hitting her.

"Well, you just let me know if there are any changes you want made in the way I run things here," Helen continued in the same stiffly polite tones. "Tanner has always eaten breakfast in the kitchen. Says it's more efficient. He doesn't have to wait for me to remember to pour him more coffee. He says for now he plans to continue to have breakfast in here. He figures you and Michael won't want to be eating as early as him. But he's left orders that lunch and dinner will be in the dining room from now on, since you'll all be eating as a family."

Rebecca caught the expression of concern on Mabel's face and realized that the sisters were worried about their positions in the household and how they would change because of her. "Whatever arrangements Tanner has made are fine with me," she said. Her gaze traveled from one sister to the other. "And as far as I'm concerned, you're both doing excellent jobs. I see no reason to change anything."

Mabel breathed an audible sigh of relief while Helen merely nodded, then turned her attention to cleaning the skillet.

For the next few minutes a peaceful calm fell over the room while Rebecca ate hungrily. To her surprise, Helen actually smiled with satisfaction when she turned and saw the empty plate. "Would you like some more?"

"Just coffee," Rebecca replied, already rising

from the table. "And," she added pointedly, "I'll get it myself. I'm not used to being waited on."

An expression of approval spread over the housekeeper's face. "You'll fit in just fine here," she asserted.

I don't fit in at all as far as Tanner's concerned, Rebecca amended mentally. Outwardly, she merely returned the housekeeper's smile, then poured herself some coffee.

As Rebecca reseated herself beside Michael, Helen approached the table with a sheet of paper. "I thought we'd go over the week's menus," she said, sitting down across from Rebecca.

Rebecca was just about to tell the woman that whatever she had planned was fine with her when there was the sound of a car approaching the house.

"Wonder who that could be?" Mabel said, glancing toward the front of the house.

"Only one way to find out," Helen replied, already out of her chair and heading toward the door.

Feeling the need to escape to someplace private for a while, Rebecca got to her feet, also. "I'll take Michael upstairs and wash off the flour," she said, offering a hand to her son.

"I'll do that." Mabel quickly rose also.

"Really, I'd like to," Rebecca insisted.

Mabel nodded knowingly. "I'll just follow you

up and get my knitting, then," she said, as Rebecca did a preliminary cleaning of Michael's hands before helping him off the stool. "But don't you let him tire you. Whenever you want a rest, you just call me. That's why I'm here."

The trio was on their way down the hall when the doorbell rang. They heard Helen answering it.

"I just had to come by to meet the new Mrs. Tanner," a woman's husky voice drawled.

"More likely to cause trouble," Mabel muttered.

Rebecca read the anxiousness on the woman's face. Whoever this caller was, Mabel didn't trust or like her.

A catty edge entered the visitor's voice. "Guess it must be unpleasant for you, Helen, dear, to have your authority usurped after all these years."

"Don't bother me none," Helen replied coolly. "I just work here."

"If you want, I'll take Michael on upstairs," Mabel said in lowered tones, clearly not wanting to make the visitor aware of their presence. "Or we can both take him up the back way. I'll get Helen to tell that witch you're napping."

Rebecca was tempted to accept the offer. There was no reason for her to meet any of the neighbors, anyway. She wouldn't be staying. But before she could act, a tall, shapely redhead entered the hall.

Rebecca guessed she was in her mid-twenties, maybe a little older. Her jeans were skintight, and her blouse was opened a button too many for real decency. "Thought I heard voices," the newcomer said. She smiled broadly and extended a hand toward Rebecca. "You must be Tanner's new bride. I'm Lynn Chambers. My family owns the adjoining ranch. I was in Houston on a shopping spree. But when I heard you'd arrived, I immediately flew home. I thought the two of us should meet."

"I was under the impression you were Lynn Galenna at the moment," Helen interjected dryly before Rebecca could respond. "Or, after three divorces, are you having trouble remembering your married names?"

Continuing to extend her hand toward Rebecca, the redhead rewarded the housekeeper's jab with an indifferent shrug. "I've decided to take back my maiden name."

Instinctively, Rebecca didn't like this woman. She noted that the smile on Lynn Chambers's face didn't reach the woman's green eyes. Instead of being friendly, they were regarding Rebecca as if sizing her up for battle. However, accepting the handshake seemed like the only polite thing to do. "I'm Rebecca," she said civilly. It could be that the redhead and Helen just didn't get along and that was what was causing the air of hostility, she reasoned.

Barely acknowledging Rebecca's response, Lynn Chambers broke the handshake quickly and shifted her gaze to Michael. "Cute kid. Guess there's no mistaking who the father is. He looks just like Tanner."

Rebecca's attempt to give the visitor the benefit of the doubt vanished. There was no mistaking the note of animosity in Lynn Chambers's voice that suggested she'd hoped there was some question as to Michael's parentage. The hairs on the back of Rebecca's neck bristled. Mabel had been right. This woman had come to cause trouble.

"Mrs. Tanner is recovering from a serous accident," Helen said curtly. "I'm not sure she's ready for visitors."

"She looks healthy enough to me," Lynn rebutted, a challenge sparkling in her eyes as they shifted back to Rebecca.

Rebecca stiffened. This female wasn't going to intimidate her. "Of course I'm strong enough for visitors," she said firmly. Releasing Michael's hand, she gave him over to Mabel. "Would you take Michael upstairs and clean him up?" she requested.

Mabel gave her a worried glance. Then, as if she

saw herself protecting Michael from the line of fire, she led him away.

"It's hotter than Hades out there," Lynn was saying, giving her long, thick tresses a flip with her hand. "Bring me a tall iced tea, Helen. We'll be on the patio."

Rebecca scowled. This might not be her home for long, but at the moment she was mistress here. "We'll be in the living room," she stipulated and taking the lead, moved with authority down the hall.

In the living room, Lynn roamed slowly among the chairs and tables, pausing to look at photographs and touching figurines as if they were old friends. She reminded Rebecca of a cat restaking a claim on what it considered its territory. A strong sense of annoyance grew within Rebecca. She'd already admitted to herself that she and Tanner had no real marriage and none of this was hers, but it didn't belong to Lynn Chambers, either.

"I have the feeling you didn't come here for a neighborly chat," she said, her patience growing thin.

Lynn turned and again raked a critical gaze over Rebecca. The corners of her mouth tilted upward. "How perceptive of you."

Rebecca had never thought a smile could look so

vicious. But she'd touched death and she'd faced Tanner. This mere mortal didn't frighten her. "What do you have on your mind?"

Malicious amusement glistened in Lynn's eyes. "A warning." Picking up a photograph of Tanner as a teenager, she ran her finger along the outline of his face. Her features softened and a dreaminess replaced the amusement in her eyes. "Tanner and I have been lovers off and on for several years."

Rebecca felt as if she'd been punched in the stomach. This shouldn't have come as a shock, she admonished herself. She'd known he wasn't celibate. *I just never expected anyone to make this kind of announcement to my face,* she reasoned to explain the intensity of her reaction.

"And as you must know, he's very pleasing to be with." Setting aside the photo, Lynn smiled salaciously. "I like to think I'm partially responsible for that."

"I suppose practice does improve one's performance," Rebecca replied with a coolness she didn't feel. Recalling her inexperience, she guessed Tanner must have been bored by her almost immediately. The guilt he'd felt because she'd been a virgin was probably the only reason he even remembered her.

"However, I didn't come here to discuss Tanner's prowess in bed,'' Lynn continued, barely acknowledging Rebecca's response. She frowned disgruntledly. ''We both know he only married you because of his son. Tanner is not the marrying kind. At times that has been frustrating to me. In moments of anger I've sworn off him and gone out and found myself a husband. But other men eventually bore me and I come back to Tanner.'' Her frown deepened. ''I suppose I could have entrapped him like you did by getting pregnant. But I didn't consider that fair.''

Rebecca glowered. ''I did not entrap him. This marriage was his idea.''

Lynn raised a disbelieving eyebrow, indicating she considered that statement ridiculous. ''Anyway, I thought it would be only neighborly to warn you that I don't intend to give him up. You can stay and act as his brood mare if that pleases you. I've never been fond of the idea of bearing children myself, and he apparently does want them at whatever cost.'' An acridness in her voice insinuated she thought the cost of being married to Rebecca was a bit high. ''However, my bed will always be available to Tanner, and I do expect him to join me on a fairly regular basis. We've always enjoyed each other's company immensely. I suppose as long as you don't mind sharing him, we'll all get along just fine.''

Listening, Rebecca had no doubt that the woman meant exactly what she said. It also occurred to her that it was because of Lynn Chambers that Tanner felt no urgency to claim his marital rights. The woman was beautiful and sensual. And he must know that any time he wanted companionship it was available. If Rebecca had harbored even the tiniest illusion about this marriage working, it was gone now.

"Well, I never!"

Rebecca glanced toward the door to discover Helen standing there with the glass of iced tea.

"Your pappy should have taken you over his knee years ago," the housekeeper continued grimly, shaking her head disapprovingly. "I don't believe I've ever heard anything so shameful—except maybe on one of those soap operas."

"Now, Helen, I know you adore Tanner. But you have to admit he's no saint," Lynn chided with an amused grin. A maliciousness suddenly entered her eyes and she swung her attention back to Rebecca. "But then, it would appear neither is his wife."

Rebecca colored with embarrassment at this blatant reference to her one-night affair with Tanner.

"Well, I never!" Helen repeated with an even stronger disapproval.

Lynn laughed. "We're adults here, Helen. Surely you must have figured out that Michael wasn't an immaculate conception."

Rebecca's embarrassment gave way to cold anger. She'd had enough of the redhead. Making a mental note to extract a promise from Tanner that Michael would not be exposed to the woman, she pointed toward the door. "I think it would be best if you left," she said with firm dismissal.

Rewarding Rebecca with an icy glare, the redhead took the glass of tea from Helen. As if asserting her right to be there, she took a leisurely sip. "It's not up to your usual par," she informed Helen haughtily, as she handed the nearly full glass back to the housekeeper. Then moving unhurriedly down the hall, she said over her shoulder, "I think I'll just go find Tanner first and let him know I'm back."

Rebecca's hands balled into fists. She most definitely wasn't going to stick around and be the brunt of ridicule—the silly little wife who waited at home while her husband was out with his sexy lover.

"That girl needs a swift kick," Helen muttered. Her attention turned to Rebecca. "I know you're still recovering from your accident and I know it's none of my business, but a wife who shares her husband's bed has an advantage. Like I said yesterday, I don't know what there is or was between you and Tanner. But I do know that he's a man worth fighting for.'' Having made this pronouncement, she strode off in the direction of the kitchen.

''Provided he wants to be fought for,'' Rebecca said quietly, wandering over to the window and looking out at the arid landscape. But he didn't. At least not by her. Her resolve firmed. She'd never been one to hang around where she wasn't wanted. Nor would she allow anyone to make her look like a fool.

From the front of the house, she heard the sound of a car door closing and then a car driving away. Going out into the hall, she saw Tanner coming in. There was a large red lipstick smear on his cheek. Rebecca's stomach knotted and a coldness filled her. ''I see Ms. Chambers found you,'' she said dryly.

''Yeah,'' came his terse reply as he used the sleeve of his shirt to give his cheek a swipe.

He looked more irritated than guilty. *I guess he was hoping to keep her a secret from me,* she decided. She felt like an idiot. It infuriated her to admit it, but deep inside she had harbored an infinitesimal hope that this marriage might work. *But you knew it wouldn't,* she admonished herself for this still-existing touch of insanity. And coming here had served its purpose. It had cured her of him. All she felt for him now was disdain.

"Tell Helen I'll be ready for lunch around noon," he said, pausing to pull on his boots in the hall, then continuing toward the stairs. "I want to take a shower first."

A cold one, no doubt, Rebecca mused acidly watching him take the stairs two at a time. She bet herself that he'd find some excuse to leave the house that night to spend time with Lynn Chambers. Well, she wasn't going to stay there and play the fool!

Her jaw set in a resolute line, she mounted the stairs. He'd already entered his room and shut the door by the time she reached the landing. But she was in no mood to be deterred. Striding over to the wooden barrier, she gave it one sharp knock, then entered, only to be narrowly missed by his dusty, sweat-soaked shirt as he flung it onto a chair.

Surprise registered on his face. He paused with his hands on the metal button of his jeans.

This time the sight of his bare chest only stirred self-directed anger within her. "I'm calling an end to this farce of a marriage. I want you to arrange for Michael and me to fly back to Idaho Falls today,'' she ordered. Then, without waiting for a response, she started to leave.

But before she could make good her escape, he caught her by the arm. Jerking her back into his room, he kicked the door shut. ''I don't consider giving our marriage less than a day a fair chance.''

She glared up at him. Did he think she had no pride? The thin hold she had on her control snapped. ''A fair chance? Your lover came here this morning to inform me that as far as she's concerned she sees no reason for the two of you to discontinue your affair. Then you come into the house with lipstick on your face, a very large clue that you agree with her, and you have the nerve to say I'm not willing to give this marriage a fair chance? What kind of an idiot do you think I am? I will not stay here and have people laughing at me behind my back.''

She paused, her anger mounting. ''Or, considering the bluntness I've encountered, maybe they'll just laugh in my face.'' She tried to jerk free but his hold on her tightened.

''Lynn is not my lover, nor has she ever been,'' he growled. ''She's a spoiled brat who enjoys causing trouble.''

That she actually wanted to believe him infuriated Rebecca even more. Her gaze shifted to his cheek, the readable cynicism on her face calling him a liar. "I suppose you were only being polite when you walked her to her car and kissed her goodbye."

He released her, and his expression hardened in anger at the accusation in her voice. "She came down to the corral and said she wanted to congratulate me on my marriage. I was coming back up to the house, so she walked with me. When we got to her car, she started to kiss me. The action caught me unaware. I turned away and she got me on the cheek." He shook his head at his stupidity. "I should have known she was up to something." His eyes narrowed on Rebecca as if he could will her to believe him. "I've never lied to you. We may not have a great deal in our favor, but I was hoping you trusted me. I figured you had to have some faith in me, since you were willing to leave Michael in my care if you'd died."

Rebecca drew a shaky breath. Every instinct told her that he was telling her the truth. Now she felt like a total fool. In a moment of frustration and anger, she'd barged in here sounding like a jealous wife. "I do believe you," she said stiffly. Wanting only to escape, she took a step toward the door. "I'll see you at lunch."

She could feel him watching her as she reached

for the knob. Then her hand froze in midmotion. The fact that Lynn Chambers wasn't his lover didn't really change anything. Her jaw tensing with purpose, she turned back toward him. His expression was shuttered, giving no indication of what he was thinking. "I still see no reason for my staying any longer," she said. "I'm not dim-witted. I know you don't really want me here. There's no place for me in your life."

Impatience spread across his features. "Of course I want you here. As for a place in my life, you're my wife."

She matched his impatient scowl with one of her own. "I'm not a wife. At least not by my definition. I'm a woman who's living across the hall. Someone who's only here because you want your son here. And, judging from your behavior last night, someone you can barely stand to be alone with."

She'd thought, after her outburst about Lynn, she couldn't be any more embarrassed than she already was. But as she heard what she was saying, she realized she was wrong. She had to get out of there before she said anything else. But as she turned and reached for the door, Tanner again captured her by the arm.

"The reason you're across the hall is because I promised your aunt and uncle I'd give you plenty of time to complete your recovery. And I promised you I wouldn't force you into anything you weren't ready for," he said gruffly. He turned her to face him fully. His expression was one of grim control. "I heard you last night because I couldn't sleep. All I could think about was you alone in that big bed." Releasing her arm, he ran his fingers along the line of her jaw. "You have no idea how hard it was for me to leave you." A bitter smile curled one corner of his mouth. "I remember when I first saw you at Cactus Anne's. I'd never felt such a strong attraction for any woman before. I thought it would fade through the years, but it seems to have remained strong."

He was admitting his feelings toward her were no more than physical, but then she'd always known that. Her own hope that her attraction to him had lessened at least a little with time was dying in the heat of the fire he was igniting within her now. But then, that was one of the reasons she was here. Surely this fire wouldn't continue to burn this hotly once she'd grown more used to his lovemaking, she reasoned.

Leaning forward, he kissed her lightly. "If you're not ready for this to go any further, you'd better tell me now," he warned huskily.

For one brief second she considered being coy.

But it was only an instant's hesitation. There was no sense in lying about the desire he kindled within her. "If we're going to try to make this marriage work, we might as well start now," she replied.

He needed no further encouragement. Within moments her shirt had joined his on the chair. Deserting her mouth, he kissed her shoulder, then trailed kisses downward as he knelt in front of her and began unfastening her jeans.

A passion so strong that she ached for him to hurry invaded every fiber of her being. Then, abruptly, unexpectedly, he abandoned his task. Beneath her palms she felt the muscles of his shoulders stiffen. With his hands resting on her hips, he straightened away from her. Following the line of his vision, she saw him looking at the long scar across her abdomen left from the operation that had repaired her internal injuries.

Her ardor cooled. It would seem that his attraction has been cured, she thought, attempting to ignore the knot of hurt and embarrassment forming in her stomach. Then pride glistened in her eyes. Well, she was cured, too. She could not remain attracted to a man who was so shallow.

Wanting only to get away from him as quickly as possible, she lifted her hands from his shoulders and started to step back, away from his touch.

His hold on her hips tightened and his gaze shifted to her face. She froze. There was no revulsion in his eyes. There was only concern and frustration.

"I don't want to do anything that will harm you," he said through clenched teeth.

The blue of his eyes was dark like the sky before a storm. Seeing the strain his control was costing him, the coolness that had invaded her vanished as the fires reignited. "I've had enough time to heal," she assured him.

He grinned. "You don't know how glad I am to hear that." Leaning forward, he nipped her side gently, then reapplied himself to removing her clothing....

Later, standing in the shower scrubbing his back, Rebecca chewed her bottom lip. She'd hoped being with him wouldn't be as exciting as it had been the first time. But it had been. He'd made certain she'd enjoyed herself, and afterward, he hadn't just left her. Nor had he allowed her to leave him.

"I still haven't had my shower," he'd said, kissing her on the shoulder a few minutes after their bout of lovemaking. "You could join me." The mischievous grin returned. "Isn't it a wifely duty to wash your husband's back?"

"I suppose it could fall into that category," she'd replied, his gaze warming her like the sun on a hot July day.

Just then a knock had sounded on the bedroom door and she'd stiffened feeling like a kid caught with a hand in the cookie jar. Then she'd scowled at herself. She and Tanner were married. Still, she was glad Tanner had locked the door to ensure their privacy.

"Tanner, are you coming down to lunch soon?" Helen's voice sounded through the wooden barrier. An edge of concern entered it as she added, "And have you seen Rebecca? I can't find her any-where."

"Yes, I've seen Rebecca," Tanner called back, casting an exaggeratedly leering gaze along the line of Rebecca's unclothed body.

"Maybe I should go on down to lunch," Rebecca suggested in hushed tones. She knew it was silly, but she felt wanton being in Tanner's bed in the middle of the day.

"Oh, no, you shouldn't." He laid an arm across her waist, holding her in place. Returning his attention to the housekeeper in the hall, he called out, "We'll be down to have some lunch after a while. Don't wait for us."

Rebecca flushed as she glanced toward the door and wondered what Helen would think.

"Well, it's about time you two started acting like husband and wife," the housekeeper called back with approval. In the next moment, they heard her footsteps heading toward the stairs.

"Agreed," Tanner replied in a low growl, playfully nipping Rebecca's earlobe. "And now it's time for you to wash my back."

"Apparently a wife's work is never done," she'd bantered back, allowing him to pull her with him off the bed and toward the bathroom.

Now as she soaped his back then moved to his chest, she felt like giggling. This was more fun than she could ever remember having. But instead of laughing, she schooled her face into a mock expression of having been imposed upon. "Since I've been doing all the work so far, you'll have to dry us," she stipulated.

He raised a playfully quizzical eyebrow. "I don't believe I've ever heard of that being a husband's duty."

"I've always believed that married couples should share the chores," she tossed back.

An unexpected seriousness descended over his features. "Then you've got yourself a towel man," he said. "Because I'm willing to work to make this marriage a success."

"I'm willing to work for that, too," she admitted.

He smiled. "Then I'd say we have a fighting chance."

Rebecca wished he hadn't made it sound like so fierce a battle. Again she reminded herself that their marriage wasn't something he'd chosen freely.

"And," he continued, kissing her lightly, "since it's easier to win a battle with a united front, I think it's time you moved from across the hall and into my bed."

As he spoke he'd been trailing his hands along her sides and down over the curve of her hips. Desire again grew within her. *As long as I don't start counting on this marriage succeeding, it can't hurt to try,* she reasoned. *And it can't hurt to enjoy myself in the process,* she added. "I've always thought husbands and wives should share the same bedroom," she conceded huskily.

He drew her more securely against him. "Then consider yourself moved in." His touch became more possessive. "Lunch is going to have to wait a little longer...."

"I was beginning to wonder if I should take a tray up to you," Helen said, with an amused gleam in her eyes, when Tanner and Rebecca finally came down to the kitchen for lunch.

"Helen, really!" Mabel admonished as Rebecca's cheeks reddened.

A mischievousness Rebecca had not thought the housekeeper was capable of showed on the woman's face. "Newlyweds need their sustenance," Helen replied, her gaze focusing on her sister. "I'm sure you remember."

This time it was Mabel whose cheeks reddened. "Really, Helen," she repeated, clearly at a loss for any other comeback.

"They also need to be in the same bedroom," Tanner said. His voice took on a note of command. "I want Rebecca's things moved into my room today."

To Rebecca's surprise, instead of immediately moving to obey Tanner, the housekeeper turned toward her. "Are you agreeable to that?" she asked. "Not that I think you shouldn't be, but I made your aunt a promise to look after your welfare."

It seemed that everyone had made numerous promises to Susan, Rebecca mused. She caught Tanner watching her. A question flickered in his eyes as if he was wondering if she'd changed her mind. Deep down inside a little voice warned that it might be safer if she did, but she ignored it. She met his gaze levelly. "I'm quite agreeable," she replied.

Helen drew a breath of relief. Glancing toward her sister, she said, "Since Michael's napping, Mabel, and you've got time on your hands, you can serve them their food. Everything's cooked, so you can't ruin it. I'll go get Sally and Leigh working on moving Rebecca's things immediately."

"My cooking isn't that bad," Mabel called after her sister's retreating back. "My husband didn't die of starvation."

"Those two," Tanner muttered as he and Rebecca went into the dining room. "They keep life from getting dull."

Rebecca glanced up at him. The crooked grin she saw on his face caused a lump to form in her throat. It was obvious he genuinely liked the women. Suddenly she found herself wishing he liked her as much. *Don't go getting your hopes up,* she warned herself.

To her surprise, during the meal he talked to her about the work he planned to do around the ranch that afternoon. There was an uneasiness about him when he first began to talk as if he wasn't certain she would be interested. But Rebecca *was* interested. In fact, she was shaken by how strongly she wanted to know as much about him as possible. She told herself this was only for Michael's sake and because she'd agreed to try to make this marriage work.

Tanner's uneasiness faded. It didn't go away entirely, and she guessed he wasn't any more certain of the outcome of their relationship than she was. Still, as they ate and talked, it occurred to her that this was the sort of conversation a real husband and wife would have. When he finished and started to leave the table, he paused by her chair and dropped a kiss on top of her head.

For several minutes after he left, she sat drinking her coffee and staring at his empty chair. She couldn't deny that the old attraction was as strong as ever. It might only be physical, but it had a hold on her. A wistfulness entered her eyes. Maybe this marriage *would* survive.

That, however, appeared to be a minority opinion, she discovered when she went upstairs a little while later. Reaching the landing, she heard Sally's and Leigh's voices coming from her room.

"Guess Jim just lost the pool. He was sure she wouldn't last two days," Sally was saying.

"Any fool would've known she'd have lasted longer than that," Leigh returned. "Only an idiot would walk out on a place like this and all of Tanner's money.''

"She did once before," Sally pointed out.

"Yeah," Leigh admitted. Her voice became slightly catty. "Truth is I was beginning to wonder about Tanner's reputation. I thought maybe some of those stories about how much fun he could be were made up. You know how some women like to talk. And, he hasn't been dating hardly at all since his daddy died."

"He's been real busy," Sally said in Tanner's defense. "And him getting her into his bedroom so fast is proof he hasn't lost his way with women."

"That means you think they might actually make a go of this marriage?" Leigh asked, skepticism strong in her voice.

Sally gave a short laugh. "No. Marriage is hard enough when two people are in love. I just figure it's going to take a little longer for the two of them to get bored with each other now." An impishness entered her voice. "Truth is, if I wasn't so in love with Mike, I wouldn't mind giving Tanner a try myself. He's a hunk."

"Yeah," Leigh agreed. "My guess is that he'll get tired of her before she gets tired of him."

"Have you made a wager in the pool yet?" Sally asked.

"I had them down for seventeen days," Leigh admitted. "But I think I'll change it to thirty-four."

"I figure on seven months even," Sally said with confidence. "I'd have taken five, but Tanner's got staying power, and if he wants something to work, he'll give it a while. 'Course when he put her in a separate room, I figured I'd lost for sure. But this move changes everything."

"You're right about that," Leigh agreed. "I'm definitely going to change my bet. But I still think seven months is too long."

"And I think those two need a lecture on discretion," Helen's voice sounded from behind Rebecca.

Turning, she saw the housekeeper mounting the stairs. It occurred to her that discretion was not the housekeeper's strongest point, either, but she chose not to make this observation aloud. Instead, she said, "My mother always told me that if there were things I didn't want to hear, I shouldn't eavesdrop."

Gasps came from the doorway of the bedroom where Leigh and Sally had been working. Glancing in that direction, Rebecca saw the two women standing there, their faces red with embarrassment. Determined to handle this with dignity, she turned back toward the housekeeper. "Have you taken out a bet?" she asked with schooled casualness as if she found this interesting but of little concern.

Helen scowled at the two women who were staring mutely, then shifted her attention back to Rebecca. "I never make wagers on affairs of the heart. They're much too unpredictable." Her gaze shifted back to the women behind Rebecca, and her expression became stern. "Besides, I have better things to do with my time. Seems like to me the two of you do, too."

"Yes, ma'am," both women said in unison and returned to their task.

The walls seemed to be closing in around Rebecca. "I think I'll go for a walk," she announced, and changing direction, went back downstairs and out the front door. Standing on the porch, Helen's words came back to her. The housekeeper had referred to the situation between Rebecca and Tanner as an affair of the heart. "That's precisely what I mustn't let it become for me," Rebecca said, her jaw set in a hard line. She was more convinced than ever that was one sure way of getting hers broken.

And, she added with determination, *I'm bound to get tired of him as quickly as he gets tired of me.*

Chapter Eight

Four days later, Rebecca stood in the middle of the living-room floor. She had nothing to do. Following the daily routine he'd established, later that afternoon, when he was finished with work, Tanner would come and take her and Michael riding. After that, the three of them would eat dinner together and then play until it was Michael's bedtime. The brown of her eyes darkened with remembered passion as a soft smile played at the corners of her mouth. And, once Michael was tucked in, she and Tanner would play.

Abruptly the memory of their shared passion faded and the smile vanished. The problem was, she was finding it difficult to fill the major portion of her daylight hours. Helen, Sally and Leigh took care of all the household chores. And while Michael certainly occupied some of her time, those hours only involved playing with him. Mabel did all of the work.

A look of resolve spread over Rebecca's face. Leaving the house, she went in search of Tanner. As she strode past one of the corrals, she noticed a couple of cowboys stop what they were doing and watch her. The speculative expressions on their faces made her wonder if they were in the betting pool. When one gave the other a nudge, she guessed that they were. Knowing her expression wasn't exactly friendly, she guessed that the one who'd given the nudge had a low number.

Shrugging off the thought, she continued toward the barns. Tanner came out leading his mount when she was still some distance away. The smile of greeting that had appeared on his face when he first saw her faded as he approached her.

Out of the corner of her eye she saw the ranch hand who had nudged his friend earlier give his friend an even firmer nudge.

"You look like a woman with something on her mind," Tanner said when he reached her.

"I don't have a place here," she said bluntly. "I feel like a fifth wheel. I serve no real purpose."

He regarded her with an impatient scowl. "You're my wife. The house is your responsibility, and so is Michael."

Rebecca disagreed. "Helen runs the house like clockwork. I suppose we could fire Mabel and I could take over the complete care of Michael, but I like her and she loves him. Besides, even if he was my full-time responsibility, I'd still have time on my hands."

Reaching up, he trailed a gloved finger along the line of her jaw. "I'm willing to take up a little more of that time."

The sudden deepening of the blue of his eyes caused her legs to weaken. She couldn't believe how, with just a look, he awakened her desire. To her chagrin, she was forced to admit that instead of growing bored with him, she craved him more each day. But as inviting as this offer was, she knew it wasn't a practical solution. "You have a ranch to run," she pointed out.

"How about taking up knitting or crocheting?" he suggested. "My mother used to enjoy doing those, and I noticed Susan does, too."

Rebecca glared at him. "I've worked all my life, Tanner. I need a job, not a hobby."

"You're supposed to be spending your time regaining your strength," he argued reasonably.

She shook her head at his obtuseness. Frustration filled her. Then a sudden realization struck her. The reason she felt out of place here was because there was no place for her here. *You knew that when you came,* she reminded herself. But this time, it hurt. Deep down inside, she wanted to belong here. *You're letting your body do your thinking for you,* she chided herself. Unable to continue facing him, she said stiffly, "I'd better get back to the house. Michael should be waking soon." Turning away, she strode quickly toward the house.

Again she noticed the two cowboys by the corral and saw the one nudge his companion again. "Could be he's won his bet," she muttered under her breath. The fear that she was going to get hurt badly if she stayed was growing by leaps and bounds. If she was smart she'd pack and be gone by nightfall.

Rebecca was halfway across the patio when she heard steps on the flagstones behind her. In the next instant Tanner's hand fastened around her arm, bringing her to an abrupt halt.

"Do you know how to work a computer?" he demanded.

Startled, for a moment she simply stared at him.

"Well, do you?"

"Yes," she replied, wondering what that had to do with anything here at his ranch.

"Then come with me."

It wasn't as if he'd given her a choice, she thought as he continued to maintain his grip on her arm while he guided her through the living room, down the hall and into his study. Once there, he released her. Then, crossing to the far wall where a large piece of furniture that looked like a cabinet sat, he opened it. Inside was an elaborate computer setup. "My tax accountant talked me into this a year ago. He said doing my taxes would be easier for him if I'd start keeping my records in this thing. But after a couple of looks at the instruction manual, I decided it wasn't for me. If I remember correctly, you have a degree in accounting." He waved his arm toward a bookcase behind a large oak desk on the other side of the room. "My records are there. If you want to try to organize them into this thing, you're welcome to do it."

She knew he considered this busy work, just something to keep her occupied. But he had understood her need to do something she considered productive. And he was attempting to help her find a place for herself here at his ranch. Again it occurred to her that it would probably be smarter for her to simply leave today, but the will wasn't there. Instead, she said, "It'll feel good to be back at a computer keyboard again."

Relief showed on his face. Removing his hat, he bowed in a cavalier manner. "Consider this machine your domain." Straightening, he kissed her lightly on the tip of her nose. "Never saw a woman's eyes light up at the sight of office equipment before," he added with a shake of his head and a crooked grin as he headed toward the door.

Alone in the room, she faced the machine. "He thinks of you as a toy he's using to appease me," she informed it. Her mouth formed a thoughtful pout. "Shall we show him what you can do?" She shrugged. "Might as well. We don't have anything else to do."

The pout twisted into a quirky grimace. "Holding one-sided conversations with a computer that isn't even turned on is a definite sign I need to get back to work." Pulling over a chair, she sat down at the console and flipped on the switch.

"Did you find everything you needed to work with the computer?" Tanner asked at dinner that evening.

Michael had been holding the center of attention talking about the lizards and the cattle they'd seen

on their late-afternoon horseback ride. Startled that
Tanner had even remembered, she glanced toward
him, certain he was only asking the question out of
politeness. But to her surprise there was honest interest in his expression. "I just spent the time I had
today getting acquainted with the system," she replied. "Once I start compiling data, I'll be needing
more disks."

"Make me a list and I'll see that you get whatever you need," he instructed. Then, winking at
Michael, he turned their conversation to his plans
for their ride the next afternoon. "Tomorrow," he
informed his son in a businesslike manner as if the
boy were one of his regular hands, "we'll check
out the herd of cattle grazing on the north range."

Michael responded gleefully.

Watching them, Rebecca realized that Tanner
was already grooming their son to follow in his
footsteps. *And now he thinks he's found a nice little
niche for me, too.* This thought should have irked
her, but instead, she found that she didn't mind the
idea of fitting into his world. The problem was she
couldn't help wondering if someday he might regret
tying himself to her merely for the sake of their
child. There was always the chance that he could
meet someone else and fall in love. Her stomach
knotted painfully. Pride came to her rescue. *Or I*

*might meet someone I'll fall in love with. Someone
with whom the attraction won't be simply physical.
The trick is to think of this marriage as a legal
affair with the strong possibility that one of us will
want out sooner or later.*

But during the next days, she found herself growing more and more comfortable in her niche within
Tanner's world. "Dangerously comfortable," she
informed the chart on the screen in front of her one
afternoon. And it was Tanner's fault.

She'd expected him to treat the work she was
doing with an air of indulgence. She hadn't expected him to behave as if he considered it really
important.

But beginning on her second day with the computer, he'd come in asking questions. With each
succeeding day, his manner had become more and
more businesslike toward her work until there was
no doubt in her mind that he considered what she
was doing an asset. "And that's making it very difficult for me to keep in mind that he had to find a
place for me here," she muttered. "That I didn't
really belong...that I still don't really belong...that
I'm only here because I'm Michael's mother."

"Are you cursing the machine or my record
keeping?" Tanner's voice interrupted.

Jerking around she saw him entering. He was dressed in jeans and a blue cotton shirt, and he smelled of horses. He tossed his hat and gloves onto a chair as he strode toward her. Watching him, her pulse quickened. He most definitely could live up to any reputation he'd earned in his younger days. "Neither," she replied, glad he hadn't been able to hear exactly what she'd been saying. Again, wishing she didn't find him so attractive, she turned back to the machine and added with forced nonchalance, "Some women talk to their small appliances. I talk to my computer."

"Sounds to me like you've been working too hard," he said, coming to a halt behind her chair. Leaning down, he kissed the nape of her neck.

Just this once, show a little immunity, she ordered herself.

"Maybe you should quit early today," he suggested, trailing kisses to the hollow beneath her ear while he massaged her shoulders.

Her body ignited. *I'll only feel frustrated if I don't give in to this,* she admitted. Besides, how could she get bored with him if she didn't participate, she reasoned, dismissing the command she had just given herself. "I suppose it wouldn't hurt to relax a little," she conceded huskily.

"Relaxing wasn't what I had in mind," he replied, easing her chair around until she was facing him. Kneeling in front of her, he began unbuttoning her blouse.

She had hoped that she might experience just a twinge of boredom. But only excitement stirred within her. He was now tossing her bra onto the chair with her blouse. As his tongue gently flicked a hardened nipple, she gasped with delight. "You do have a very effective way of disrupting a person's work schedule," she admitted huskily.

"Never thought seeing a woman sitting at a computer could be so enticing," he replied, rising and pulling her to her feet with him. "But then, I've always found you enticing."

For one brief moment she was certain she saw accusation in his eyes, as if he felt caught in a situation in which he didn't want to be. Then the flicker of discontent was gone. In its place was passion and purpose. His hands flattened against her back and he began massaging the suddenly taut muscles.

The thought of pushing him away played through her mind. It was only her body that interested him. But the work-roughened texture of his palms sent a thrill surging through her, and the fire he could kindle so easily within her flamed into life.

As long as I don't think of him as any more than

a warm body to please me, there can't be any harm in enjoying him while this marriage lasts, she reasoned, beginning to unfasten the buttons of his shirt.

Chapter Nine

Several weeks later, Rebecca was sitting on the floor of Michael's room with her son in her lap. She was reading him a story before putting him to bed for his afternoon nap. Unexpectedly, Helen entered the room followed immediately by Mabel.

"Please come with me," the housekeeper requested.

"I'll finish reading Michael his story," Mabel added quickly.

Rebecca had never seen the housekeeper like this. It was obvious that, for Michael's sake, Helen was attempting to present a calm front, but there was open anxiety in her eyes.

"Yes, of course," Rebecca replied, fear sweeping through her at the thought that Tanner might have been injured. Forcing herself to pause long enough to give Michael a hug and kiss, she turned him over to Mabel and followed the housekeeper out of the room.

"I didn't know if I should bother you," Helen said uneasily as they descended the stairs. "But I figured a wife should be with her husband at a time like this."

Rebecca saw Leigh and Sally standing huddled in the hall, conversing nervously. They both turned toward her, and the anxiousness she'd seen in Helen's eyes was reflected on their faces. "What's going on?" she demanded.

"It's Gray Knight, Tanner's father's horse," Helen replied, coming to a halt at the foot of the stairs. "He's been gored by that new bull Tanner just purchased. He's going to have to be destroyed. Tanner's in the study now getting his gun."

Rebecca's gaze swung toward the study door just as Tanner emerged. She'd never seen him look so stricken and so grim; and there were tears in his eyes. He looked like a man who had just lost his best friend. Her gaze shifted to the rifle he carried. "Tanner, let someone else do it," she said, moving toward him.

He looked at her as if he couldn't believe she had the nerve to make such a suggestion. "I have to know it's done right," he snarled. "It's a duty I owe my father." Rebecca saw his jaw twitch as he fought to maintain control over his emotions. "He loved that horse," he added gruffly as he passed her on his way toward the back door.

Rebecca knew that it wasn't just Tanner's father who had loved that horse. Tanner cared for the old stallion just as strongly. Her gaze shifted to Helen. "He can't do this," she said in a voice that sought the housekeeper's help.

Helen's expression became even more anxious. "He has to," she replied with a catch in her throat.

Rebecca turned to Sally and Leigh with a silent plea.

"It's his duty," Sally said in a voice barely above a whisper while Leigh nodded in confirmation.

The pain Rebecca had seen in Tanner's eyes tore at her. She couldn't let him face this alone. "His sense of duty seems to constantly put him into situations he'd rather avoid," she muttered, running after him.

He was halfway to the corral by the time she caught up with him.

"Go back to the house," he ordered without

even glancing at her, his attention remaining focused on his destination.

"I will not," she replied, jogging to keep up with him. Ahead of her she saw a group of cowboys gathered inside the corral near the prone body of the old stallion. Among them was Jim Gordon, Tanner's foreman. "Let Jim do it," she pleaded.

Coming to an abrupt halt, he glared at her. "This is something I have to do, Rebecca. And it needs to be done quickly, before the animal suffers any more. Now go back to the house." Without waiting for a response, he again started toward the corral.

Rebecca scowled at his departing back. The man had a stubborn streak a mile wide. But she could be just as stubborn. Catching up with him, she fell into step beside him.

He scowled down at her impatiently.

"It's a wife's duty to stand by her husband at times like this," she said, her jaw set in a resolute line.

"It's not a pretty sight, Rebecca," he warned.

She felt the pain she saw reflected in his eyes as if it were her own. "I can handle it," she assured him, continuing beside him. But her confidence was only external. Inside she was shaking. Still, she couldn't leave him. If he needed her, she wanted to be there for him.

"Let me do this for you, Tanner," Jim said as Tanner and Rebecca entered the corral.

"It's something I've got to do," Tanner replied.

Rebecca saw the uneasiness on the cowboys' faces as their gazes shifted from Tanner to the horse and then to her. A silence fell over the group.

The stallion whinnied weakly. "Goodbye, old boy," Tanner said quietly. Taking a position in front of the horse, he lifted the rifle and fired.

For a full minute no one moved. Rebecca barely breathed as she watched Tanner staring down at the animal. The rifle hung limply at his side. A tear trickled down his cheek. "Stupid animal," he growled in a voice barely above a whisper. "Why couldn't you have been happy in your corral?"

"I only took my eyes off him for a minute," a young cowhand said from Tanner's right. "I was carrying feed in to him. Never thought he'd get out so quickly and go visiting."

Rebecca saw Tanner's free hand ball into a fist. He turned, fury on his face.

The young cowhand stood stiffly waiting for the blow, as if he felt he deserved it. He looked nearly as upset about the horse's death as Tanner did, and Rebecca felt sorry for him. She was also scared. Tanner was a strong man. If he did take a swing at the cowhand, he was sure to hurt him.

The knuckles on Tanner's hand whitened and his back stiffened. He drew a terse breath and swung his gaze back to the horse. "Accidents happen," he said gruffly. Then he started back toward the house.

Rebecca trotted beside him. It occurred to her that he might want to be alone, but she needed to make certain he was all right before she left him.

His pace slowed. She expected him to tell her to go away, but instead, he said, "My father taught Gray Knight to open gates. Said it saved him from having to dismount all the time."

Rebecca had known the horse knew this trick. It had caused trouble before. Gray Knight's own enclosure had a special latch the stallion couldn't unfasten.

"Who'd have thought that horse would be so stupid as to go into a corral with a skittish bull?" he continued grimly.

The anger she'd seen him control when he hadn't hit the young cowhand returned to the surface. As if it was too strong to be held inside, it etched itself deep into his features. His jaw formed a decisive line. They had reached the back patio. Abruptly he halted, then turned so sharply he almost collided with her. "That damn bull!" he raged. He started back toward the corrals.

Fear for him flooded through Rebecca. Racing

after him, she grabbed his arm, forcing him to stop. "Where are you going?" she demanded.

"An eye for an eye," he growled, jerking free and continuing back in the direction from which they'd just come.

Momentarily she stood frozen. He was going to kill the bull. In a way, she could understand. He hurt too much. He wanted to strike back at something. But she knew he was a good man and later his conscience would make him pay. She ran after him. "Tanner, you can't. It isn't right," she argued, falling into step beside him.

"That bull killed Gray Knight. Why should he live?" he snarled.

Again she grabbed his arm, forcing him to stop. "Because he's a dumb animal. He was acting out of instinct."

Out of the corner of her eye she saw the cowboys watching them. Jim started toward her and Tanner, but Tanner glared at him warningly and the foreman stopped in his tracks. Ignoring Rebecca's argument, Tanner jerked free again and continued to where the bull was penned.

Rebecca glanced at Jim. He gave a shrug as if to say that once Tanner's mind was made up, there was nothing anyone could do. Her gaze shifted to Tanner. She knew he would hate himself if he went through with this. Again she raced after him. He'd reached the corral by the time she caught up with him. "Tanner, please. Don't do it," she pleaded, placing her hand on the wrist of his hand that held the gun. "You'll regret it."

For a long moment he stood staring at the bull. As if the animal sensed danger, it backed to the opposite side of the enclosure, its eyes on Tanner, its head lowered and poised for battle. Then in a barely audible voice, Tanner said gruffly, "You're right."

Rebecca, still holding on to his wrist, felt his muscles relax. His expression, however, remained taut. The anger was still strong, but even more there was pain and sorrow. Turning away from the corral, he began to walk, not toward the house but toward the vast open range beyond the barns and corrals.

Again, Rebecca wondered if she should leave him alone. But she couldn't make herself turn away. Instead, she followed a couple of paces behind.

He walked until the ranch enclosure was a mere dot on the flat, arid landscape. Ahead of them, she saw a large boulder. Tanner stopped when he reached it and stood staring at it.

Uncertain of her welcome, Rebecca watched in

silence for a long moment. Quietly, she asked, "Tanner, are you all right?"

He glanced over his shoulder. The surprise of seeing her there registered on his face. "Yeah, I'm fine," he replied, returning his attention to the boulder.

But he didn't look fine. He looked tired and sad. She stood there trying to think of something to say. She wanted to approach him, put her arms around him and hold him and help him with his pain, but she wasn't certain he wanted her comfort.

"Some people," he said gruffly, unexpectedly breaking the silence between them, "believe that a horse reflects his rider."

The image of Tanner on his black stallion played through Rebecca's mind. Both were strong-willed and proud. "I suppose that could be so," she replied.

"My father was as stubborn, foolish and bull-headed as Gray Knight."

Rebecca studied his taut profile. Now she understood. It wasn't the death of the horse that was tearing at Tanner. It was something to do with his father. She took a step toward him. "I remember you were very fond of your father," she said evenly.

"I wanted him to live," Tanner growled, his gaze never moving from the boulder. "But he refused to follow the doctor's orders. After his heart attack, they told him to take it easy. There was nothing they could do to repair the damage, but he would have lived several more years if he'd taken better care of himself. They might as well have been talking to this rock. I found him here late one afternoon. I'd been out checking fences. While I was gone one of the wranglers came in with a report of spotting mountain-lion tracks on the north range. A cat would only have been there if he was hunting for food. Instead of waiting for me to get back, my dad decided to go have a look for himself. I figure the heart attack hit him just a few feet from this boulder. He managed to dismount and sit himself in the shade. Then he died—alone.'' Anguish etched itself into Tanner's features. "I should have been at the house. I should have stopped him from coming out here."

Again Rebecca felt his pain as if it were her own. Unable to stop herself, she approached him and laid a hand on his arm. "You can't blame yourself for his death."

He turned toward her. "I know," he conceded. "But I wasn't ready to lose him." His expression became shuttered. "I know there are times when you must resent me for forcing you to come here.

But Michael is all I have left, Rebecca. I can't give him up without a fight.''

She wished she did resent him. But she didn't. Standing there with him, she could no longer deny her true feelings. She'd fallen in love with him. That was the last thing she'd wanted to do, but it had happened, anyway. "I don't resent you," she said. "I understand how you feel."

"I don't know if I should really believe that," he replied, "but I appreciate you saying it." He drew a tired breath, then nodded toward the ranch enclosure in the distance. "Guess we'd better be getting back."

"Guess so," she replied, again falling into step beside him as he turned and started back. It hurt that he wasn't in love with her. But she couldn't fault him for that. He'd never claimed to be.

He slipped his arm casually over her shoulders. "Hope that bull knows how grateful he should be to you," he said, then added, "I'm grateful, too."

A small shaft of pain shot through her. It wasn't his gratitude she wanted. But he needed a friend right now, and that was what she would be. She slipped her arm around his waist as they continued toward the house in silence.

"I knew if anyone could help him through that, you could," Helen said.

On their return to the house, Rebecca had stopped in the kitchen to get them some iced tea while Tanner returned the rifle to the study.

"I had my doubts about your marriage when you first came here," Helen admitted as she fixed the drinks.

"Really, Helen," Mabel said, issuing her usual scolding from her seat at the table.

Helen received it with the usual impatient glance, then continued, "But I can see it's going to work out just fine."

Rebecca wished she had the housekeeper's confidence. Forcing a smile, she accepted the drinks and carried them into the study.

Tanner was standing staring out the window. When she entered, he turned toward her. "I'm glad you're here, Rebecca," he said simply.

She knew he only meant it as one friend to another, and her stomach knotted. She wanted him to mean much more.

Late that night, she lay watching him sleep. Dismay mingled with consternation. How could she have been so foolish as to fall in love with him? That was the one thing she'd warned herself not to do. It wasn't as if he were perfect. He had his faults. But then, so did everyone.

A wistfulness spread over her features. Maybe he would fall in love with her.

Her jaw firmed. There was no reason he couldn't. He wanted the marriage to work. She would be a good wife. It could happen.

A gleam sparked in her eyes. She could court him, subtly, of course. She wasn't very practiced in womanly wiles, but she did have an advantage. She was already his wife.

Chapter Ten

The next morning Rebecca sat in bed, her arms wrapped around her legs with her chin resting on her knees. She was watching Tanner as he stood at the sink in the adjoining bathroom shaving.

Ask him, she ordered herself. She hadn't been this nervous since she'd been a teenager and was trying to get up the courage to ask George Kelps to the annual Sadie Hawkins dance at school. By the time she'd gotten her courage up, he already had a date. She'd been embarrassed and had sworn never to participate in another event where the girl asked the boy for a date.

But this was different. She had no competition. Nothing ventured, nothing gained, she told herself.

"I was wondering," she said, as he turned off the water and began toweling his face dry, "If you'd like to go on a picnic today?"

He hung the towel back on the rack and returned to the bedroom. "I've got a lot of work that needs to be done," he said apologetically.

I can't even get a date when there's no competition. She forced a smile. "Sure, I understand." Pride caused her to add, "Actually I've got an idea for a new chart I want to punch into the computer, anyway." He had paused with one arm in his shirt and was studying her. Afraid he might read the disappointment on her face, she lowered her gaze, picked up the magazine that lay on her bedside table and began to leaf through it.

"'Course Jim could handle what needs to be done," he said, thoughtfully. "Sure, why not? I'd be happy to go on a picnic with you and Michael this afternoon."

Rebecca forced herself to look up at him. A catch formed in her throat and she cleared it nervously. *Go on, say it,* she ordered herself. *If he refuses to go with you alone, then you'll know this is futile and you won't have to put yourself through this agony again.* "I was thinking that we'd leave Michael here. That just you and I would go."

Surprise registered on his face, then his expression became shuttered. "Sure. We can leave around eleven."

Her pulse began to race. He'd accepted! *Act nonchalant,* she ordered herself. "Fine," she said, returning her attention to the magazine. But her mind refused to focus on the page in front of her. She felt like a teenager going on her first date. "There's a recipe in here I want to show to Helen," she heard herself saying, too nervous to remain totally silent. *Don't start rattling on like you're one brick short of a load,* she warned herself, and clamped her mouth shut.

Thumbing through the magazine for the fictional recipe, she heard him moving around the room, but she didn't dare look up. She was afraid he might read how much his acceptance meant to her. *You've got to get a grip on yourself,* she ordered. It wasn't as if this were a life-or-death situation. *It just feels like it is.*

"See you at eleven," Tanner said, pausing in the doorway on his way out.

Be cool, she ordered herself. Looking up, she smiled stiffly. "Eleven."

A puzzled expression played across his face. Then he shrugged it away. "Have a good morning," he added, and continued on out.

What she had was a nervous morning. She felt

guilty about not bringing Michael along on the picnic, so she gave him added attention.

"Now, don't fret about the boy," Mabel admonished her. "Husbands and wives need private time together. He and Helen and I'll have our own picnic on the patio."

When Tanner arrived back at the house, she half expected him to insist they take Michael along. But he didn't, and at a few minutes past eleven, she and Tanner rode off alone.

"There's a mesa on the south range," he said as they left the barns and the corrals behind. "Thought we could have our picnic in its shadow. Then if you feel up to it, we could climb to the top. The view's nice."

"Sounds terrific." The moment these words were out, a wave of self-consciousness swept through her. There had been too much enthusiasm in her voice. She'd sounded like a giddy adolescent. Maybe he hadn't noticed, she thought hopefully. She glanced toward him. His jaw had tensed and she knew he had.

Capturing her horse's reins, Tanner brought both mounts to a halt. "You're acting like a skittish colt," he said, studying her narrowly. "What's wrong, Rebecca?"

She released a sigh. This was not going well at

all. Instead of causing him to develop warmer feelings toward her, she was making him irritated. "Nothing's wrong," she said.

Impatience etched itself into his features. "It's obvious something's bothering you."

She felt frantic. She hadn't planned this outing to make him angry. Pride wouldn't allow her to tell him the whole truth, so she settled for half. "I just thought it was time for us to get to know one another better." That sounded ridiculous, she chided herself. She'd been sharing his bed for more than two months now. "Not that we don't know one another fairly well already," she amended in a rush. "I admit that we do know one another very well in some respects—" She stopped abruptly and flushed. He was scowling at her now. No matter what she said, it only seemed to make matters worse.

For a long moment he regarded her in silence, then his expression became neutral. "You're right. There's a lot about each other we don't know." Releasing her reins, he gave his horse a nudge and they continued to ride toward the south.

Now I know what people mean when they say, "The silence was deafening," she mused. They hadn't spoken for the past ten minutes and she wanted to scream from the pain of the stillness between them. "How did your morning go?" she asked, hoping that some casual conversation would ease the tension.

He gave an indifferent shrug. "It went fine."

Don't stop now, she ordered herself. *It can't get any worse.* "Did you get that fence mended?" she persisted, recalling that Helen had mentioned he'd said something about a break in one of their fences.

He glanced toward her and she knew he'd guessed her ploy. But this time he helped keep the conversation going. He answered her query about the fence with more than a cursory yes and then asked her about the chart she'd mentioned putting into the computer.

She sensed he wasn't really interested in talking, but she wasn't willing to go back to their silence. *Guess he didn't realize how hard he'd have to work to make this marriage a success,* she thought unhappily. How could she have made such a mess of this picnic so quickly? Well, she'd just have to make the rest of it something he'd want to remember.

By the time they reached the mesa, she was calmer and more in control. *This courting business is going to take time,* she told herself. *I've got to relax.*

They spread their blanket out in the shade cast

by the mesa and ate. During the meal, she managed to keep a pleasant conversation going. But periodically she'd catch a glimpse of Tanner shifting his shoulders as if his muscles were tense. *No doubt he's bored out of his mind,* she decided.

She considered attempting to seduce him, but the moment never seemed right. *You've got to make your own moments,* she told herself. *Be romantic. Be inventive. Be spontaneous. Isn't that what all the magazines suggest to win and keep your man's love?* But just as she was about to act on this thought, an armadillo slowly toddled across her line of vision, and she caught a glimpse of a scorpion as it crawled behind a nearby rock. *No sense in rushing things,* she decided.

"How about if we try that climb," Tanner suggested as he finished the apple he'd been eating.

Glad for any physical activity, she nearly bolted to her feet. It was not an easy climb, but she didn't mind. Anything was a welcome relief from the mental debating she'd been doing with herself about whether to disregard all the crawling things and seduce him, anyway.

Reaching the flat, hard surface, Rebecca drew a deep breath. For the first time in hours, her muscles weren't knotted with tension. They were too tired to be.

Tanner came and stood beside her.

"It's beautiful up here," she said with honest enthusiasm, scanning the hot, arid landscape stretching out on all sides.

For a long moment Tanner didn't respond, then he said stiffly, "We've talked about the ranch, Michael and the weather. We've both agreed that Helen is an excellent cook. We've climbed for half an hour. You've seen the view. Now do you want to tell me what's really on your mind?"

Looking up at him, she saw the guardedness in his eyes. It occurred to her that at this rate, by the end of the day she would have created a chasm between them so wide it could never be breached. "I guess I'm not very good at asking personal questions," she said. "But I was being honest with you. I just thought it would be a good idea for us to get to know one another better."

Tanner didn't look convinced. "What do you want to know about me?"

Everything was the response that popped into her mind, but that would make her sound like a lovesick idiot. *Think of something innocuous to begin with,* she directed herself. *Ask him what his favorite color is.* But instead she heard herself saying, "I've been wondering why you never married." She flushed when he raised a quizzical eyebrow. "I mean before you felt you had to marry me because of Michael,'' she elaborated. This was not going at all the way she'd planned. *So much for subtlety,* she chided herself. Still, this was one of the questions uppermost in her mind.

He stared off into the distance. ''I considered getting married once, but she walked out on me. Guess she thought I wasn't very good husband material.''

Rebecca's stomach knotted. So he had been in love once. She did have competition. To make things worse, she was competing with a memory, and memories had a way of not being very realistic. Mentally she groaned. She was trying to win him away from an idealized woman.

''What about you, Rebecca?'' he asked, breaking into her thoughts.

She frowned in confusion. ''What about me?''

He was studying her now. ''Why didn't you ever get married?''

Nervous under his gaze, afraid she might reveal more than she wanted, she turned and feigned intense interest in a bird circling overhead. ''I guess I just never found the time to look for anyone. Then, after I discovered I was pregnant with Michael, he occupied all my time.'' That was what she'd always told herself in the past. But the truth was she'd never found anyone who attracted her as strongly as Tanner had.

His hands closed around her upper arms and he turned her toward him. "I know I wouldn't have been your first choice, Rebecca. But I'm trying my best to make this marriage work out for all of us."

I wouldn't have been your first choice, she corrected mentally. Aloud she said, "I would like for us to be a family, too, Tanner." She just wished he didn't look as if he considered the task Herculean.

But he must feel as if it is one, she thought later that night as she lay beside him in the dark. She'd spent the rest of the afternoon and evening trying not to think about his lost love. But the shadowy image kept popping into her mind. Watching him playing with Michael, she'd found herself wondering if Tanner, once in a while, pictured the woman he'd wanted to marry in her place. That thought had been difficult enough to deal with.

But to make matters worse, that night in bed, when he turned to her, she found herself wondering if he was pretending she was the other woman. Not only was she merely a warm body, but a surrogate warm body! That hurt too much. She couldn't relax. A coldness permeated every fiber of her being. The fires he could normally so easily start refused to ignite.

"I've never enjoyed one-sided participation," he'd said at last. He'd muttered something about the climb up the mesa obviously being too tiring. Then turning away from her, he'd gone to sleep.

Now she lay there alone on her side of the bed staring at the ceiling. Hot tears filled her eyes. She'd begun the day wanting him to fall in love with her and she'd ended it by pushing him away. *You idiot!* she screamed at herself. *You're letting a phantom from his past destroy your future.*

Turning on her side, she stared at his broad back. The thought of reinitiating their lovemaking played through her mind. But he was already asleep. And she was tired. Besides, she hadn't been able to entirely rid herself of the thought of him pretending she was his unrequited love, and she didn't want another disaster the same night. *By morning I'll have vanquished her from my mind,* she promised herself. And a little early-morning lovemaking would be a pleasant way to start the day.

But the next morning she awoke alone. She glanced at the clock. It was still early. She hadn't overslept. Her gaze shifted to the bathroom. It was empty. In the dim dawn light she could see that the jeans Tanner had tossed over the back of the chair the night before were gone. Then she heard it—water running in the guest bathroom across the hall.

Leaving the bed, she grabbed her robe and pulled it on as she left the room. Reaching the door of the bathroom, she knocked lightly.

Tanner, his face half-covered with shaving cream, opened it. "Thought I'd gotten out of the room without waking you," he said, returning to the sink to finish shaving. "You were so tired last night and you slept so restlessly I figured you could use some extra sleep."

She told herself that he was just being thoughtful, but there was a subtle undercurrent in his manner that made her feel unwelcome. "That was very considerate of you," she managed levelly. He was probably a little miffed about last night, she reasoned. Men's egos were supposedly a bit sensitive where their sexual prowess was concerned. *Entice him back to bed,* she commanded herself.

"You still look exhausted," he observed, continuing to concentrate on his shaving. "Why don't you go back to bed and get some more sleep?"

He was politely but bluntly telling her to go away and leave him alone. For a moment she considered doing just that, but this rift between them was her fault and she didn't want it to go on. He had finished shaving and was rinsing off his face. His shirt was hanging on a hook on the door. She forced a playfulness into her manner. "If you want your shirt, you'll have to come get it," she said, taking the shirt from the hook and making a quick retreat back to their bedroom.

Cursing her clumsiness, she managed to get out of her robe and nightgown and was pulling his shirt on by the time he finished drying his face and followed.

Seeing her with his shirt half on and half off, the impatient expression on his face changed to one of amused interest. "Guess you aren't as tired as I thought," he said.

"Guess not," she returned, her heart pounding rapidly. The blue of his eyes had darkened to a shade of midnight. *Don't mess this up,* she ordered herself. And she did try to keep it playful. But all during their lovemaking she couldn't stop worrying about whether or not she was satisfying him as much as the woman he'd wanted to marry could have. Uncertainty and the desperate wanting to please him made her anxious.

When it was over, she was as tense as when they had begun.

Tanner didn't look pleased, either. His jaw was set in a taut line as he left the bed.

Well, I've succeeded in convincing him I'm no

fun anymore, she chided herself, watching him dress in silence.

Buckling his belt, Tanner headed for the door, but with his hand on the knob, he stopped. Turning, he retraced his steps back to the bed. He looked down at her grimly. "I'm not sure what this morning was all about. If you did it to appease me because you weren't in the mood last night, then it was unnecessary. My ego isn't tied to how many times a day, week, month, or year I have sex with a woman." His expression grew even grimmer. "And I don't like to feel that I'm merely being accommodated. If my partner isn't enjoying herself, then I don't enjoy myself."

"I wasn't trying to merely accommodate you," she replied in her defense. "I'm just a little uptight. I thought I could relax..." She stopped. He was looking grimmer by the moment. Nothing she said was improving the situation.

"I've got work to do," he said gruffly, and stalked out of the room.

Rolling over, she buried her face in the pillow and let out a low groan. Nothing she'd said or done for the past twenty-four hours had worked out right. "Because I care too much," she moaned. "I've got to back off and reapproach him slowly," she instructed herself.

But reapproaching Tanner began to appear impossible. He avoided being alone with her throughout the entire day. That night when they went to bed, he went immediately to sleep.

The next morning he was up and shaving when she awoke. Lying there watching him, she wanted to be in his arms, but she was afraid to make a move toward him. She was terrified it would turn into another disaster.

As if he felt her watching him, he glanced toward the bed. "Morning," he greeted her stiffly when he saw that she was awake.

"Morning," she returned, forcing a smile. He didn't look very happy to see her, and the fear that these past two days had convinced him this marriage wasn't going to work spread through her.

Finishing shaving, he rinsed his face and toweled it dry. Then, pulling on his shirt, he reentered the bedroom. "Been thinking," he said as he buttoned the garment. Pausing, he looked at her. "I don't want you to feel you're a prisoner here at the ranch. Maybe it'd help if you got away for a week or two. I'll make arrangements for you and Michael to go visit your aunt and uncle. I suspect you're a mite homesick for them."

Without giving her a chance to respond, he left.

Rebecca lay staring at the spot he had occupied.

He hadn't asked her if she wanted to go. He'd ordered her to go. She wondered which of them he'd really meant when he'd made the reference to feeling like a prisoner.

"Going off isn't any way to solve a problem," Helen said when Rebecca entered the kitchen a little later. "I know something's been wrong between you and Tanner these past couple of days, but the two of you can't work out your problems if you're hundreds of miles apart."

Rebecca's jaw tensed. Pride refused to allow her to admit that her leaving was Tanner's idea, not hers. "There's nothing to work out," she said. "It's just that I've been a little homesick, so I'm going to visit my aunt and uncle for a couple of weeks."

"This is your home now," Helen pointed out, clearly refusing to buy that explanation. Her expression became one of a person giving stern but motherly advice she felt should be heeded. "All married couples have their little spats. What you've got to keep in mind is that it's always better to clean a wound than to let it fester."

Rebecca was in no mood for this. Where was Mabel when she needed her?

As if in answer, she heard Michael jabbering. Glancing toward the pantry door, she saw her son emerge followed by Mabel, who was carrying a jar of peaches. But instead of berating her sister for interfering, Mabel frowned worriedly. "Helen's right. I sure would hate to see one of those cowboys win that pool."

So would I, Rebecca replied mentally. Aloud she said, "Michael and I are just going away for a short visit." She regarded the sisters with a cool indifference she didn't feel. "It's perfectly natural for a person to visit their relatives periodically."

The sisters exchanged glances but said no more.

As soon as she had eaten, Rebecca called Susan. If Tanner wanted her out of his house for a while, then she would leave as quickly as possible. Susan was delighted to hear from her. But when Rebecca asked if she could come visit immediately, her aunt's voice became filled with concern.

"Has something happened?" she asked worriedly. "I thought the last time we talked, you sounded happy."

"I really don't want to talk about it now," Rebecca replied. However, the thought of having Susan to confide in buoyed her spirits. Maybe this trip was a good idea, after all. Maybe she wasn't really even in love with Tanner. Maybe it was an infatuation. Getting away from him might solve all her problems.

After getting Susan's okay for the visit, she went ahead and made arrangements for her and Michael to leave that afternoon. When Tanner came in to eat lunch, she told him of her plans.

"I'll fly into San Angelo to see you off," he said. "I'm sure you'll have a good time."

Rebecca felt a jab of disappointment. She'd hoped he'd show a little remorse about her departure. He could have at least said he hadn't expected her to leave so quickly, she fumed. He didn't even seem upset about Michael's leaving. Maybe he was getting tired of playing daddy, she thought. Maybe he wouldn't care if they never came back at all.

But at the airport in San Angelo, she knew she was wrong about his not caring about Michael any longer. The way he held the boy when he said goodbye convinced her that he found parting with his son difficult.

Setting Michael down, he drew her into his arms. "And I'll see you in two weeks," he said firmly.

There was no question that this was an order. But she knew he was only demanding her return because she and Michael came as a pair. "Two weeks," she replied evenly.

Chapter Eleven

"Well, are you ready to talk yet?" Susan asked.

Rebecca had just finished putting Michael down for his afternoon nap and returned to the living room where her aunt was sitting knitting.

Setting her knitting aside, Susan regarded her niece with motherly concern. "You're very good at putting on a cheerful face for your uncle. But I know those nervous little tics of yours. Something is bothering you. You've had a day to recover from your trip, Michael's asleep, and Jack's at work. We won't be disturbed."

"I do need to talk to you. I intended to when I came," Rebecca admitted. "I'm just not sure where to begin."

"Can I assume this has something to do with Tanner?" Susan prodded. She frowned anxiously. "He hasn't begun to mistreat you, has he?"

Rebecca shook her head. "That I could handle. I'd leave and never look back." She breathed a frustrated sigh. "The problem is I've fallen in love with him."

Susan's expression relaxed. "Considering the fact that you're married to him, I would think that's an advantage."

The frustration in Rebecca's eyes deepened. "It would be if he loved me or I thought he could learn to love me."

"And what makes you think he doesn't or can't?" Susan demanded. "You're a bright, good-hearted, lovely young woman. Any man should be proud to be your husband."

Rebecca crossed the room and gave her aunt a hug. "And you're prejudiced," she said with a smile. "But you do help keep my spirits up."

As Rebecca moved away, Susan rose. Drawing herself to her full height, her hands on her hips in an authoritative stance, she regarded her niece sternly. "I know I'm prejudiced. But I'm also practical and, I repeat, there's no reason why he shouldn't fall in love with you."

Rebecca's stomach knotted. It had to be said.

Maybe if she got it out into the open, she could deal with it better. "Yes, there is. He's in love with someone else."

Susan looked shocked. "How do you know that?"

"He told me." Hot tears burned at the back of Rebecca's eyes, but she refused to cry.

Anger spread over Susan's face. "After dragging you all the way to Texas insisting that the two of you try to make your marriage work, he just up and tells you that he loves someone else? I suppose he at least had the decency to ask for a divorce." The anger abruptly faded to be replaced by loving understanding. "So that's why you're here. You've come back to see if we want you." Susan approached Rebecca and put her arms around her. "You know you're welcome here. Jack and I would love having you and Michael come live with us."

Gently working free from her aunt's embrace, Rebecca took a step back and shook her head. "No, he didn't ask for a divorce. Whoever the woman is, she's in his past. He still wants our marriage to continue."

Now Susan was frowning in confusion. "You mean that this woman is no longer in the picture? Who is she? Where is she?"

Rebecca shrugged. "I have no idea." Dismay

spread over her face and she issued a frustrated groan. "That's the hard part. I feel like I'm competing with an idealized phantom. Ever since I found out about her, I've been anxious and tense. I say the wrong thing. I do the wrong thing."

"In other words, you're allowing this woman from his past to destroy your future?" Susan looked reproving. "I would think a flesh-and-blood woman by his side would interest him a great deal more than some phantom."

Rebecca grimaced. "I told myself that. I even tried to court him. But like I just said, all of a sudden I can't seem to say or do anything right."

Susan regarded her skeptically. "I find that hard to believe."

"He practically threw me off the ranch," Rebecca offered as proof. "This trip was his idea." The last statement came out filled with agitation. Suddenly realizing what she'd said and how she'd said it, she flushed. "Not that I didn't want to see you and Uncle Jack," she added quickly, now worried that she might have alienated her aunt. Groaning again, she shook her head. "There, you see? Everything I say comes out wrong."

"You are a little uptight," Susan agreed. Smiling, she gave Rebecca another hug. "But you don't have to worry about my feelings. I know what you meant.''

Rebecca breathed a grateful sigh. "Thanks."

"Now to the solution to your dilemma." Susan's expression again became stern. "Is Tanner worth fighting for?"

The cowboy's image loomed in Rebecca's mind. "Yes," she replied unequivocally.

"Then I suggest that is precisely what you do."

Rebecca chewed on her bottom lip. "I'm just not sure how."

"You'll think of something," Susan assured her with a bright smile.

"I wish I had your confidence," Rebecca returned wistfully. Abruptly her jaw firmed. "However, if I'm going to fight for him, there's no sense in wasting time. I hope you won't be offended if I cut this visit short."

Susan gave an approving nod. "You should be with your husband." Hugging Rebecca tightly, she added, "And if Tanner doesn't fall in love with you, then there's something wrong with the man."

Rebecca went to make the arrangements for her flight back to the ranch. But when she started to dial the number there to arrange for Tanner to send the plane to San Angelo for her, she stopped. She needed to see the look on his face when she showed up unexpectedly. It would tell her a lot about whether he really wanted her there or not. She had her pride. She wouldn't fight for a lost cause.

Calling the airlines, she made reservations for herself and Michael on an early-morning flight the next day. Then she arranged for a charter to fly her from San Angelo to the ranch.

The next morning Jack and Susan drove her to the airport. "The man's a fool if he doesn't fall in love with you," Jack said with certainty as he gave her a hug goodbye. "But in case he is, you've got a home with us whenever you want it."

As she gazed out the window of the plane a little later, she muttered, "And I may have to take him up on that. At least until I can find a job and a new apartment." She wanted to believe Tanner could learn to care for her, but she had strong doubts.

By the time the chartered plane touched down at the ranch, she was exhausted. Not only had the trip been a long one but it had been an anxious one. She'd played a hundred scenarios over in her mind and still had not been able to decide on a way to begin successfully wooing Tanner.

"Daddy," Michael said cheerfully as they disembarked at the end of the runway nearest the house.

But it wasn't Tanner who came driving up in the

Jeep to meet them. It was Fred Riley, one of the hands.

"Welcome, Mrs. Lathrop," he said politely, as he loaded her and Michael's luggage into the vehicle. "Didn't know you were returning so soon."

She saw the curiosity in his eyes and wondered if he had a bet in the pool, too. "We came back a little early," she replied noncommittally.

"The boss is in San Angelo. He should be getting back before dark, though," he informed her as they drove toward the house.

As much as she wanted to see Tanner, Rebecca was relieved that she would have a little time to recuperate from her trip. *As if that's going to help,* she thought dryly. Trying to fight a new wave of nervousness, she concentrated on Michael. He was talking excitedly about seeing his pony.

"It's good to have you back," Helen greeted her at the door.

"Tanner hasn't slept well at all since you left," Mabel added as they all entered the house. "He's been up pacing in his study till all hours."

Probably wondering how much longer he can endure our marriage, Rebecca mused. Outwardly, she forced a smile. "I thought I'd change and take Michael down to the stables to see his pony. He could use the fresh air and exercise after being in planes and airports all day.''

''I'll do that,'' Mabel said quickly. ''Why don't you freshen up a bit and then rest until Tanner gets home?''

''You could use a bit of fixing up. It never hurts to look your best for your man,'' Helen added more bluntly.

Rebecca caught a glimpse of her image in the mirror. She did look haggard. ''You've got a point,'' she replied, handing Michael over to Mabel.

''You really could be a little more tactful,'' she heard Mabel admonishing Helen as the two escorted the boy toward the kitchen.

''Rebecca's a forthright person. She doesn't need any sugarcoating. I'm going to miss her if this marriage doesn't work out,'' Helen replied.

''I'll miss you, too,'' Rebecca admitted under her breath, realizing how fond she'd grown of the two sisters.

A little later as she stood in the shower, the memory of showers taken with Tanner played through her mind, and a lump formed in her throat. Just being away from him for two days had been difficult. ''I'm really going to miss him if this doesn't work out.'' Her jaw firmed. She could make him happy. She just wasn't certain how to convince him of that.

After her shower, she pulled on a robe and stood in front of the closet trying to choose what to wear. The red dress was the sexiest thing she owned. She decided on it. But as she reached for it, indecision assailed her. When she tried too hard, she'd only managed to make him angry at her. Maybe she should dress simply in slacks and a sweater, or better still, jeans and a shirt, and go back to her old daily routine.

I'm too tired to think straight, she confessed to the image in the mirror, which stared back at her with dark circles under the eyes. Her gaze shifted to the bed. It wouldn't hurt to take a short nap.

Curling up under the covers, she nestled her head in Tanner's pillow. The lingering scent of his shampoo and after-shave gently filled her senses and she drifted off to sleep....

"Rebecca."

It was Tanner's voice. Groggily, she opened her eyes. In front of her were two sturdy columns housed in dark gray suit pants.

"Rebecca, it's time to wake up. Helen's going to be putting dinner on the table soon," Tanner's voice ordered from overhead.

Rebecca noted that it was neither angry nor

pleased, just neutral. Turning on her back, she looked up at him.

His expression became one of concern. "Are you sick?" he asked.

Mentally she groaned. So much for looking her best. Her fingers went up to comb her hair from her face. "I'm fine," she replied. "I was just tired."

Nodding acceptance of this explanation, he moved away from the bed.

She'd been sleeping in the nude. He'd seen her that way many times, but now she felt shy. Keeping the covers in front of her, she retrieved her robe from the foot of the bed.

The action wasn't lost on Tanner. With an impatient scowl, he turned his attention to the view beyond the window, allowing her some privacy.

Quickly she pulled on the robe, belted it, then moved toward the mirror and picked up her brush. Say something, she ordered herself. "I hope you don't mind my coming back early." She would have liked to have been wearing the red dress and to have delivered this statement in a seductive voice. Instead she was clothed in a nondescript old robe and the words came out stilted and apologetic.

He turned back toward her, his scowl deepening. "I want you to feel free to come and go at will."

She was tempted to point out that he hadn't made

her feel that way when she'd left. It had felt as if she was being thrown out. But she hadn't come back to fight *with* him. She'd come back to fight *for* him. Of course it would help if he would seem a little happier to see her. But then, she did look like something the cat had dragged in, she admitted, staring at her disheveled, hollowed-eyed self in the mirror.

"Was there a problem at Susan and Jack's?" he asked, breaking the silence that had fallen between them.

Rebecca stiffened. She was certain she'd detected a guardedness in his voice. This wasn't going well at all. She was now firmly convinced he hadn't wanted her to come back so soon. "Susan thought she might be coming down with the flu," she lied, pride not allowing her to admit that she'd come back because of him.

For a moment, he studied her in a grim silence, then he said tersely, "I went to see a lawyer today."

His words cut into her like a knife. Unable to move, she watched him in the mirror as he took a folded sheet of paper from the breast pocket of his suit jacket. Her breath locked in her lungs. He was going to ask for a divorce. At least, it will be over with, she told herself. And, I won't go making a fool of myself again. But that didn't stop the painful churning in her stomach.

"I had him draw up this document. I suppose you could call it a pre-divorce agreement. It's sort of the same concept as a prenuptial agreement. It states that if we should get a divorce, you'll have custody of Michael. I'll want some visiting privileges, but you'll have control. There are also some stipulations concerning child support. I would want to know that Michael had everything he needed. And I'd insist on paying you alimony. I'd want you to be able to devote your time to our son and not have to worry about working," he explained coolly.

Hot tears of frustration burned at the back of Rebecca's eyes. He had laid out the foundation for a divorce, but he was leaving the final decision up to her. That sense of duty again, she mused acidly. He was determined to stick with this marriage no matter how miserable it made him. Pivoting, she faced him levelly. "If you want a divorce, just come on out and say it. I thought bluntness was a characteristic of this household."

"I don't want a divorce," he said gruffly. "What I want is for you not to be afraid of me."

Rebecca stared at him in bewilderment. "Afraid of you?"

Harsh apology entered his voice. "The other day

when we were at the spot where I found my father, I know I sounded vehement about not losing Michael. I'm also very aware that the only reason you agreed to try to make this marriage work was because I threatened you with a custody battle. But I would never take Michael away from you. I know how much he means to you and you to him.''

Rebecca regarded him earnestly. ''I'm not afraid of you, Tanner. When I first came here I wasn't certain about a lot of things. But I know now how deeply you love Michael. And I know you're a fair man and a good man. It would be difficult for me, but I would feel safe sharing him with you.''

He frowned in confusion. ''I don't understand.'' Then as if he suddenly realized the truth, a bitter smile curled his lips. ''You might not be afraid of me, but when I had to destroy Gray Knight and then wanted to kill the bull in revenge, you saw a side of me you couldn't abide. That was what the picnic was all about, wasn't it? You wanted to talk to me alone. You wanted to tell me that you wanted out of this marriage, only for some reason...'' He paused. ''Maybe you're more afraid of me than you want to admit, or maybe it was for Michael's sake...you thought he should have both parents. Anyway, you didn't go through with your plan. But you couldn't bear to have me touch you. You tried to force yourself, but that didn't work.''

She watched as he drew himself to his full height. ''I never claimed to be perfect, Rebecca. I have my faults. If you can't live with them, then consider yourself free to go.'' Abruptly turning away from her, he left the room.

Rebecca stood frozen. He was wrong in his assessment of the situation, but that didn't change the fact that she had a decision to make. To stay or to leave—he'd left it up to her. She wanted to stay. But she needed some assurance that he could learn to care for her. She raced after him. The sound of his study door slamming told her where he was.

Entering the room, she found him standing with his hands gripping the mantel. ''I've never thought for one minute that you were perfect,'' she said.

Jerking around, he watched her guardedly as she kicked the door closed with the heel of her bare foot, then crossed to the center of the room.

She had done a great many difficult things in her life, but nothing had ever felt so important or so frightening. ''I have to know...'' For a moment the words caught in her throat, then she forced herself to go on. ''I have to know that you honestly want *me* to stay. Not that you want me because of Michael. But that you want me, Rebecca, to stay.''

He scowled at her. "Of course I want you to stay. We're not a family without you."

She shook her head. "That's not what I mean." Frustration gripped her. "You don't understand, Tanner. The other day—it wasn't you, it was me. I realized I was in love with you." Every muscle in her body stiffened and she paled. She'd just blurted it out! Well, at least now they could get to the truth, she told herself, attempting to be philosophical. But it meant too much to her. Her body tensed more until she felt brittle.

He regarded her with an expression of disbelief. "That doesn't make a lot of sense, Rebecca. If you're in love with me, why was it so difficult for you to share my bed the other night? You were stiff as a board. You had to force yourself to let me touch you."

Her chin threatened to tremble. She'd already bared her soul. He might as well know everything. "It was her."

The disbelief turned to confusion. "Her?"

"The other woman in your life," she elaborated, the thought of this shadowy phantom causing a sharp jab of pain.

He frowned impatiently. "There is no other woman in my life."

How could he be so thickheaded! she fumed.

"The one you told me about at the picnic. The one you really wanted to marry." Too embarrassed to continue to face him, she paced to the window and stared out with unseeing eyes as the memories of their last attempts at intimacy filled her mind. "I couldn't stop wondering if you were pretending I was her when we were together. It isn't flattering to think of myself as a surrogate lover."

"You were never a surrogate lover. You were her," he said huskily.

She turned back toward him. He was the one who wasn't making any sense. "I was her? That's ridiculous! How could I be her?"

His expression softened. "You asked me if there was a woman I'd ever considered marrying. I had considered marrying you. I'd considered it very seriously. Then you suddenly announced you'd found someone else and you vanished from my life."

A shadow of pain flickered through his eyes. "When you told me in the hospital that you hadn't wanted to saddle me with a wife you thought I didn't want, I didn't believe you. I figured you didn't think I was good husband material—that having no husband was better than tying yourself to me. I brought you out here to try to prove to you that you were wrong." A cynical half smile curved his mouth. "Or to get you out of my system once and for all."

His gaze was warming her, but she was too afraid to let herself fully believe the tenderness she saw there. Even more important, she needed to know if the attraction she read in his eyes was still merely physical or if it ran deeper. "And did you?" she asked.

He frowned. "Did I what?"

She swallowed back the lump in her throat. "Did you get me out of your system?"

Grinning lopsidedly, he shook his head as if this were the most stupid question he'd ever been asked. "That was an impossibility. The more I was with you, the more I wanted to be with you."

The blue of his eyes darkened as he moved toward her. Her pulse began to race and her legs felt suddenly weak. The fires he could so easily ignite within her were flaming into life. "Tanner, wait!" she ordered, taking a step back before he could reach her.

He frowned as if he didn't understand why she would make this demand, but he stopped.

"I can't think when you touch me," she confessed shakily. "And there's something I have to know."

He was smiling again, that charming smile that

made her want to melt in his arms. "What do you want to know?"

Maybe I should just settle for what I can have, she thought, the urge to rush into his embrace so strong it was a physical strain to remain where she was. But always wondering and worrying if he could ever care for her the way she cared for him was pure torture. *Don't give in now,* she ordered herself. "I need to know if what you feel for me is merely physical or if it's deeper, or if it's not yet deeper but you think you could learn to love me." She heard the plea in her voice but she was beyond embarrassment. It was as if her whole life hung on his answer.

The blue of his eyes darkened even more. "I've already learned to love you, Rebecca. These past two days this place has felt empty, and I've felt as if a part of me was missing. It took every ounce of control I had not to come to Idaho Falls and drag you home."

Tears of joy filled her eyes and she rushed to him. Wrapping her arms around him, she grinned up into his face. "There are going to be a lot of disappointed cowboys and cowgirls."

He frowned in confusion. "Disappointed cowboys and cowgirls?"

A mischievous gleam sparkled in her eyes.

"They've got a long wait ahead of them before anyone's going to collect in that betting pool they started."

He laughed as his hold on her tightened possessively. "A very long wait," he agreed, then met her lips with a kiss that promised forever.

*   *   *   *   *

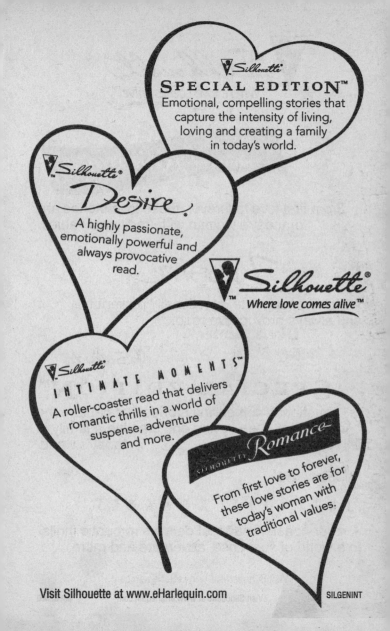